THE ARCHITECT OF FLOWERS

The Architect of Flowers

STORIES

William Lychack

A MARINER ORIGINAL
Mariner Books
Houghton Mifflin Harcourt
Boston | *New York* | 2011

For information about permission to reproduce
selections from this book, write to Permissions,
Houghton Mifflin Harcourt Publishing Company,
215 Park Avenue South, New York, New York 10003.

www.hmhbooks.com

Library of Congress Cataloging-in-Publication Data
Lychack, William.
The architect of flowers : stories / William Lychack.
p. cm.
ISBN 978-0-618-30243-7
I. Title.
PS3612.Y34A85   2011
813'.6—dc22   2010024953

Book design by Patrick Barry

Printed in the United States of America

DOC 10 9 8 7 6 5 4 3 2 1

Parts of this collection originally appeared in the following publications: "Stolpestad," in *Ploughshares;* "The Ghostwriter," in *Harvard Review* and *Open Letters,* and on National Public Radio's *This American Life;* "Griswald," in *The Sun;* "Thin End of the Wedge," in *Ascent,* originally as "Ghost Runners"; "Hawkins," in *Puerto del Sol;* "Calvary," in *The Southern Review;* "Love Is a Temper," in *Witness;* "The Old Woman and Her Thief," in *Ploughshares;* and "A Stand of Fables," in *Quarterly West.* "A Stand of Fables" was reprinted in *The Best American Short Stories 1996.* "Stolpestad" was reprinted in *The Pushcart Prize XXXIV: Best of the Small Presses.*

for Betty

There must be something very beautiful in my body,
I am so happy.

—James Wright, "Northern Pike"

CONTENTS

THE ARCHITECT OF FLOWERS

STOLPESTAD

Was toward the end of your shift, a Saturday, another one of those long slow lazy afternoons of summer—sun never burning through the clouds, clouds never breaking into rain—odometer like a clock ticking all those bored little pent-up streets and mills and tenements away. The coffee shops, the liquor stores, the laundromats, the police and fire and gas stations to pass—this is your life, Stolpestad—all the turns you could make in your sleep, the brickwork and shop fronts and river with its stink of carp and chokeweed, the hills swinging up free from town, all momentum and mood, roads smooth and empty, this big blue hum of cruiser past houses and lawns and long screens of trees, trees cutting open to farms and fields all contoured and high with corn, air thick and silvery, as if something was on fire somewhere— still with us?

1

That sandy turnaround—and it's always a question, isn't it?

Gonna pull over and ride back down or not?

End of your shift—or nearly so—and in comes the call. It's Phyllis, dispatcher for the weekend, that radio crackle of her voice, and she's sorry for doing this to you, but a boy's just phoned for help with a dog. And what's she think you look like now, you ask, town dogcatcher? Oh, you should be so lucky, she says, and gives the address and away we go.

No siren, no speeding, just a calm quiet spin around to this kid and his dog, back to all the turns you were born to, your whole life spent along these same sad streets. Has nothing to do with this story, but there are days you idle past these houses as if to glimpse someone or something—yourself as a boy, perhaps—the apartments stacked with porches, the phone poles and wires and sidewalks all close and cluttered, this woman at the curb as you pull up and step out of the car.

Everything gets a little worse from here, boy running out of the brush in back before you so much as say hello. He's what—eight or nine years old—skinny kid cutting straight to his mother. Presses himself to her side, catches his breath, his eyes going from your face to your uniform, your duty belt, his mother trying to explain what happened and where she is now, the dog, the tall grass, behind the garage, woman pointing. And the boy—he's already edging away from his mother—little stutter steps and the kid's halfway around the house to take you to the animal, his mother staying by the side porch as you follow toward the garage and garbage barrels out back, you and the boy wading out into the grass and scrub weeds. Sumac, old car tires, empty bottles, refrigerator door. Few more steps and there—a small fox-colored dog—beagle mix lying in the grass, as good as sleeping at the feet of the boy, that vertigo buzz of insects rising and falling in the heat, air thick as a towel over your mouth.

And you stand there and wait—just wait—and keep waiting, the boy not saying a word, not looking away from the dog, not doing anything except kneeling next to the animal, her legs twisted awkward behind her, grass tamped into a kind of nest where he must have squatted next to her, where this boy must have talked to her, tried to soothe her, tell her everything was all right. There's a steel cooking pot to one side—water he must have carried from the kitchen—and in the quiet the boy pulls a long stem of grass and begins to tap at the dog. The length of her muzzle, the outline of her chin, her nose, her ear—it's like he's drawing her with the brush of grass—and as you stand there, he pushes that feather top of grass into the corner of her eye. It's a streak of cruel he must have learned from someone, the boy pushing the stem, pressing it on her until, finally, the dog's eye opens as black and shining as glass. She bares her teeth at him, the boy painting her tongue with the tip of grass, his fingers catching the tags at her throat, the sound like ice in a drink.

And it's work to stay quiet, isn't it? Real job to let nothing happen, to just look away at the sky, to see the trees, the

3

garage, the dog again, the nest of grass, this kid brushing the grain of her face, dog's mouth pulled back, quick breaths in her belly. Hours you stand there — days — standing there still now, aren't you?

And when he glances up to you, his chin's about to crumble, this boy about to disappear at the slightest touch, his face pale and raw and ashy. Down to one knee next to him — and you're going to have to shoot this dog — you both must realize this by now, the way she can't seem to move, her legs like rags, that sausage link of intestine under her. The boy leans forward and sweeps an ant off the dog's shoulder.

God knows you don't mean to chatter this kid into feeling better, but when he turns, you press your lips into a line and smile and ask him what her name is. He turns to the dog again — and again you wait — wait and watch this kid squatting hunch-curved next to the dog, your legs going needles and nails under you, the kid's head a strange whorl of hair as you hover above him, far above this boy, this dog, this nest, this field. And when he glances to you, it's a spell he's breaking, all of this about to become real with her name. Goliath, he says, but we call her Gully for short.

And you ask if she's his dog.

And the boy nods. Mine and my father's.

And you touch your hand to the grass for balance and ask the boy how old he is.

And he says, Nine.

And what grade is nine again?

Third.

The dog's eyes are closed when you look—bits of straw on her nose, her teeth yellow, strands of snot on her tongue—nothing moving until you stand and kick the blood back into your legs, afternoon turning to evening, everything going grainy in the light. The boy dips his hand in the cooking pot and tries to give water to the dog with his fingers, sprinkling her mouth, her face, her eyes wincing.

A moment passes—and then another—and soon you're brushing the dust from your knee and saying, C'mon, let's get back to your mother, before she starts to worry.

She appears out of the house as you approach—out of the side door on the steps as you and the boy cross the lawn—the boy straight to her once again, kid's mother drawing him close, asking was everything okay out there. And neither of you say anything—everyone must see what's coming—if you're standing anywhere near this yard you have to know that sooner or later she's going to ask if you can put this dog down for them. She'll ask if you'd like some water or lemonade, if you'd like to sit a minute, and you'll thank her and say no and shift your weight from one leg to the other, the woman asking what you think they should do.

Maybe you'll take that glass of water after all, you tell her—boy sent into the house—woman asking if you won't just help them.

Doesn't she want to try calling a vet?

No, she tells you—the boy out of the house with a glass of water for you—you thanking him and taking a good long

5

drink, the taste cool and metallic, the woman with the boy at her side, her hand on the boy's shoulder, both of them stiff as you hand the glass back and say thank you again.

A deep breath and you ask if she has a shovel. To help bury the dog, you tell her.

She unstiffens slightly, says she'd rather the boy and his father do that when he gets home from work.

In a duffel in the trunk of the cruiser is an automatic — an M9 — and you swap your service revolver for this Beretta of yours. No discharge, no paperwork, nothing official to report, the boy staying with his mother as you cross the yard to the brush and tall weeds in back, grasshoppers spurting up and away from you, dog smaller when you find her, as if she's melting, lying there, grass tamped in that same nest around her, animal as smooth as suede.

A nudge with the toe of your shoe and she doesn't move — you standing over her with this hope that she's already dead — that shrill of insects in the heat and grass as you nudge her again. You push until she comes to life, her eye opening slow and black to you — you with this hope that the boy will be running any moment to you now, hollering for you to stop — and again the work of holding still and listening.

Hey, girl, you say, and release the safety of the gun. Deep breath, and you bend at the waist and gently touch the sight to just above the dog's ear, hold it there, picture how the boy will have to find her — how they're going to hear the shots, how they're waiting, breath held — and you slide the barrel to the dog's neck, to just under the collar, wounds hidden as you squeeze one sharp crack, and then another, into the animal.

You know the loop from here—the mills, the tenements, the streetlights flickering on in the dusk—and still it's the long way around home, isn't it? Wife and pair of boys waiting dinner for you, hundred reasons to go straight to them, but soon you're an hour away, buying a sandwich from a vending machine, calling Sheila from a pay phone to say you're running a little late. Another hour back to town, slow and lawful, windows open, night plush and cool, roads this smooth hum back through town for a quick stop at the Elks, couple of drinks turning into a few—you know the kind of night—same old crew at the bar playing cribbage, talking Red Sox, Yankees, this little dog they heard about, ha, ha, ha. Explain how word gets around in a place like this, ha, ha, ha—how you gave the pooch a blindfold and cigarette, ha, ha, ha—another round for everyone, three cheers for Gully—next thing you know being eleven o'clock and the phone behind the bar is for you.

It's Sheila—and she's saying someone's at the house, a man and a boy on the porch for you—and you'll be right there, you tell her. Joey asks if you want another for the road as you hand the receiver over the bar, and you drink this last one standing up, say good night, and push yourself out the door to the parking lot, darkness cool and clear as water, sky scattershot with stars. And as you stand by the car and open your pants and piss half-drunk against that hollow drum of the fender, it's like you've never seen stars before, the sky some holy-shit vastness all of a sudden, you gazing your bladder empty, staring out as if the stars were suns in the black distance.

Not a dream—though it often feels like one—streets rivering you home through the night and the dark, that pickup truck in the driveway as you pull around to the house, as if you've seen or imagined or been through all of this before, or will be through it again, over and over, man under the light of the porch, transistor sound of crickets in the woods. He's on the steps as you're out of the car—the lawn, the trees, everything underwater in the dark—and across the wet grass you're asking what you can do for him.

He's tall and ropy and down the front walk toward you, cigarette in his hand, and you're about to ask what's the problem when there's a click from the truck. It's only a door opening—but look how jumpy you are, how relieved to see only a boy in the driveway—kid from this afternoon cutting straight to the man, man tossing that cigarette into the grass, brushing his foot over it, apologizing for how late at night it must be.

How can I help you?

You're a police officer, says the man, aren't you?

Sheila's out on the porch now—light behind her—silhouette at the rail, she's hugging a sweater around herself, her voice small like a girl's in the dark, asking if everything's all right, you taking a step toward the house and telling her that everything's fine, another step and you're saying you'll be right in, she should go back inside, it's late.

She goes into the house and the man apologizes again for the hour and says he'll only be a minute, this man on your

lawn pulling the boy to his side, their faces shadowed and
smudged in the dark, man bending to say something to his
son, kid saying, Yes sir, his father standing straight, saying
that you helped put a dog down this afternoon.

And before you even open your mouth, he's stepping forward and thanking you—the man shaking your hand, saying how pleased, how grateful, how difficult it must have
been—but his tone's all wrong, all snaky, all salesman as he
nudges his boy to give you—and what's this?

Oh, he says, it's nothing really.

But the boy's already handed it to you—the dog's collar
in your hand, leather almost warm, tags like coins—the guy's
voice all silk and breeze as he explains how they wanted you
to have it, a token of appreciation, in honor of all you did for
them today.

It's a ship at sea to stand on that lawn like this—everything swaying and off balance for you—and before you say a
word he's laughing as if to the trees, the man saying to put it
on your mantel, maybe, or under your fucken pillow. Put it on
your wife, he says, and laughs and swings around all serious
and quiet to you, man saying he's sorry for saying that.

Nice lady, he says—and when you look the boy's milk-
blue in the night, cold and skinny as he stands next to his
father—man telling how he made it home a little late after
work that night. Was past nine by the time they got around
to the dog, he says, dark when he and the boy got out to the
field—boy with the flashlight, himself with the shovel—the
man turning to the boy. Almost decided to wait until morning, didn't we?

He nudges the kid—startles him awake, it seems—and the boy says yes.

Anyway, says the man, couldn't find her for the life of us. But then we did. Not like she was going anywhere, right? Took us a while to dig that hole, never seen so many stones, so many broken bottles.

The man turns to the house behind him, the yellow light of windows, the blade of roofline, the black of trees. He lets out a long sigh and says, What a fine place you seem to have here.

You say thanks—and then you wait—watch for him to move at you.

Any kids?

Two boys, you say.

Younger or older than this guy here?

Few years younger, you tell him.

He nods—has his hand on his boy's shoulder—you can see that much in the dark, can hear another sigh, man deflating slightly, his head tipping to one side. So, he says, like I was saying, took us a while to get the hole dug. And when we go to take the collar, the dog tries to move away from us—like she's still alive—all this time and she's still alive. All those ants into her by now, imagine seeing?

He hums a breath and runs his palm over the boy's hair, says the vet arrived a little later, asked if we did this to the dog, made us feel where you're supposed to shoot an animal, slot right under the ear. He reaches his finger out to you and touches, briefly, the side of your head—almost tender—smell of cigarettes on his hand, your feet wet and cold in the grass, jaw wired tight, the boy and his father letting you hang there in front of them, two of them just waiting for whatever you'll say next to this, the man clicking his tongue, saying, Anyway, helluva a thing to teach a kid, don't you think?

A pause—but not another word—and he starts them back toward the truck, the man and the boy, their trails across the silver wet of the lawn, the pickup doors clicking open and banging closed—one and then the other—engine turning over, headlights a long sweep as they ride away, sound tapering to nothing. And in the silence, in the darkness, you stand like a thief on the lawn—stand watching this house for signs of life—wavering as you back gently away from the porch, away from the light of the windows, away until you're gone at the edge of the woods, a piece of dark within the dark, Sheila arriving to that front door, eventually, this woman calling for something to come in out of the night.

CHICKENS

Didn't know a chicken from a duck, but had a big yard and all summer before the baby, had this strange craving for eggs, and then this urge of mine for chickens we just had to have, twenty-four chicks going *peep, peep, peep, peep,* all the way home. Blocked off the kitchen, spread newspaper, got right down on the floor with them, funny little wind-up toys scrabbling everywhere, just played and played until Bob drove into the yard. He burst out laughing, of course—and then not even laughing, really—more like scoffing at me, calling me Mother Goose, asking what exactly did I think I was doing?

Why hello to you too, my love, I said to him. And how was your day today, sweetheart?

Seriously, Anna, what's with the fricken chickens?

Guess I was thinking omelets, I told him—oh, such dreams I had for how our life would be—and I smiled up to the man, saying, Watch this. I sprinkled breadcrumbs into my palm and told Bob to just hold still a second. One, two—and *ta-dahhh!*—this bright yellow chick bouncing up into my hand, creature so soft and weightless, poor thing trembling as I brought her to my cheek, smell of hay and cedar.

That's nice, said Bob, real nice—and he nudged one of the chicks aside with the toe of his shoe—man asking what did we have in this house to eat anyway? He took a can of beer from the fridge and turned and looked tired to me. These little friends of yours, he said, not thinking they're going to stay in the kitchen forever, are they?

Actually, I said, we were hoping you'd help make us a coop.

Oh, I'll help make you a coop all right—and he leaned against the counter and drank his beer—and such an urge I had to kick him, hurt that smirk off his face, yellow chicks on the floor in every direction, and Bob asking if anyone called for him.

Told him nobody called for him. Told him his father called for him. Told him his friend Domo called for him. Told him to leave my contradictions alone, saying the Mormon Tabernacle Choir called for him, asking, Who cares who called for him? Started to gather the chicks back into the box, Bob just watching all the while as I got the birds put away, crazy things scratching at the cardboard, *peep, peep, peep, peep.*

Finally covered the box with a dishtowel to try to get them quiet, washed my hands at the sink, asked what would His Highness like for dinner this evening? He opened the refrigerator for another beer—and I smiled all fake and false when he turned to me again—Bob staring like he'd never seen me before in his life, like he'd wandered into the wrong house

14

and was standing in some stranger's kitchen, these chicks in the box at our feet, whole flock peeping their lungs raw, Bob saying, You'd think we were drowning the little fuckers, wouldn't you?

You know, I said, sometimes I just don't *like* you very much.

No kidding, he said—and he took a good long slug of beer—and I started to straighten the chairs at the table. I picked up the dishes from the floor and explained this sign I saw on the side of the road. BABY RABBITS AND CHICKENS FOR SALE, CHICKS TWO FOR A DOLLAR, farmer saying we'd be lousy with eggs by summer, the man's wife giving me a bag of cornmeal for free.

And *still*, said Bob, your happy little larks always seem to cost me something, don't they?

Could always be worse, I told him. I mean, I *have* been thinking a lot about *milk* lately. Found myself following an *ice cream truck* through town the other afternoon.

Don't even joke, he said—and he leafed through the day's mail—and how I wanted to ho-hum him right back in the face, make Bob feel the way I felt for once, make *his* chin go all quicksand, have *him* begin to cry for no reason. Like any of this would happen—Bob becoming me—him having to swallow that warm backwash of tears, chew some emotion off his mouth. Yeah, right, almost had to laugh out loud, part of me wishing to catch these feelings in the room with us, trap these emotions like birds against the walls, keep and hold and finally tame these things I felt, and then part of me needing to open the windows and let this all just fly away already.

No wonder he just stood there, Bob picking his ear, looking at his fingernail, waiting for me to settle myself down. Phone bill to open, few peeps from the chicks in the box, and eventually Bob set his beer can empty in the sink, switched on the light to the basement, said to c'mon and follow him.

Had a stack of old doors downstairs, some two-by-fours, a roll of garden fencing, and we built a pen at the foot of the patio. Nearly dark by the time we finished. Looked like a house of cards, this chicken coop all leaning and shipwrecked in the yard, chicks closed up inside with a few blankets for the night, *peep, peep, peep, peep, peep*.

Think they'll be okay? I asked.

Never know, said Bob — and he clucked his tongue and put his arm around me — and I let myself ease into that old fit of his body. Even the chicks grew quiet, world as still and smooth as a pond, and those little champagne bubbles of baby inside me again. Might have been nothing, tiny fish in my imagination, faint brush of tail toward my chest, but I took Bob's hand and pressed his palm to my stomach and held my breath for this little boy or girl to move for him.

Wasn't anything there for Bob to feel yet, though he went along much longer than I expected — and he let *me* be the one to pull away first — Bob's hand touching my shoulder as we drifted toward the house, gesture so gentle and rare that I actually stopped and turned to him in the dark, that faint crackle of saliva as he smiled, Bob asking how was I feeling by the way?

Next morning became next week became end of June became a dozen and a half roosters, one hen, and a sharp shining hatchet in our future. What started as two dozen of my sweetest little whims all sunny and cartoon-cute—*peep, peep*—soon became a nightmare of roosters all mottled and nasty and mean. Roosters crowing from dawn to dark, roosters crowing from the street, roosters crowing from the nearby yards and fences and tops of cars. Chased them home with a rake. Sprayed them from shrubs with a hose. Promised vast harm upon the birds. Swore to chop each of their ugly heads off.

Went from fragile and breathless if a single chick turned up missing—God forbid a clump of feathers by the side of the house, a string of blood in the grass—and a few short weeks later I have gone from maternal and happy to whatever is the opposite of maternal and happy. Paternal and miserable, according to the dictionary, Bob laughing out loud at the kind of luck I seemed to have, all but one of my chicks turning into roosters—*hardy, har, har*—glad to amuse him so much, pleased to give him something to joke about down at the Elks.

Wasn't funny, of course, but it got me thinking at least, and I drove myself back to the farm the next day for some clarification. Same sign on the side of the road, baby angoras and leghorns for sale, huge pen filled with chicks under heat lamps—*peep, peep,* all over again—me asking, What were the chances of someone getting so many roosters anyway? Woman looked at me—little air pocket of quiet between us—and she smiled and asked when was my baby due? Put my hands to the small basketball of my stomach—easy to forget sometimes—baby, pregnant, fact of it not always real to me yet. Still, I was *not* about to let myself be distracted now.

Mission: chickens.

17

Told her a few months, end of September, and I looked at the pen, the lamps, the chicks, and breathed deep the noise and stink, and then I asked was it even possible, all but one of my chicks turning into roosters? She smiled and said she was sorry. Really no way to tell with hatchlings, she said. Supposed to startle them, and then watch what they do by instinct, cockerels clucking and standing upright, pullets silent and crouching down. Nothing too very scientific about it, I'm afraid. And again that smile of hers, that good-witch tilt of her voice, woman saying she didn't know what else to tell me, asking if I played the lottery, because my luck was bound to change.

She gave me a carton of eggs as a gift, and I stopped at the library on the way home. Returned *Common-Sense Poultry* and *Barnyard in the Backyard (All You Need to Know About Raising Chickens)*. Took out *One Hundred Chicken Recipes for Summer, The Creative Chicken Cookbook,* and *Basic Butchering of Livestock and Game*. Stopped at the hardware store and asked where might the ax department be? Bought the sharpest hatchet, the heaviest trash bags, and the deepest aluminum baking pans. Rode through town looking for Bob, wanting that big white Impala around every corner, hoping to find him at the shopping center, at the diner, man wherever he was, doing whatever he did, me just wanting to be with him. Rehearsed how I'd ask if he happened to be in the mood for some *poultry* tonight? Had the hatchet ready to make him laugh. Had the recipe books to show him. Wanted to ask if he felt like *baked* chicken or *fried* chicken or chicken *salad?* What *kind* of chicken would he like for dinner tonight? *Bar-*

becue chicken? *Parmesan* chicken? Want to pick out some new surprise of *chicken* together?

Sometimes I'd drive the whole town like this and find him at those huge supermarket windows, Bob and his father on opposite sides of the glass like mimes, both with the same long pulls of blade, same quick swipes of chamois. Sometimes I'd go all the streets and never find him anywhere, my last hope that he'd be in the yard as I pulled in, his car waiting at home all along, hood cool, joke on me. And I'd sink a little, of course, driveway always empty when I arrived, rooster on the steps of the patio, another running out of the flowerbed, another crowing on top of the garbage barrels as I started into the house.

That underwater feel of late afternoon — no note, no dirty dish in the sink, no evidence of Bob anywhere — and back outside to the coop, the nesting boxes in the corner, that one little hen sitting nervous and watchful. Asked her how was she doing this evening — *cluck, cluck* — hatchet hidden behind my back as I reached my hand under her. No eggs, I said — and I pet the bird along that soft grain of feathers — was talking to her calm and quiet, telling her not to worry, whispering how I'd keep her safe, everything all right, everything just fine.

Left her alone and walked to the middle of the yard and started to singsong the roosters home. Tossed seed to the grass, bits of bread and crackers, my least unfavorites strutting across the lawn to me first. Cesar Romero, Rudy, Earl, The Fonz. Here you are, I cooed. Look at the nice pieces of apple I have for you.

I fed Larry right out of my hand, bird rubbing at my ankles like a cat, playing with the laces of my shoes. Scooped him up and carried him to the patio—no scratches, no struggles—could have sworn he purred as he tucked his face against my arm.

Brought the cutting board to the back step outside. Had a cooking pan, a few towels, and I held the rooster down with one hand, hatchet raised with my other, closed my eyes, and then that *chuck* of the blade as it struck. Lifted the bird by its feet and let the blood drain into the pan, his head lying there on the patio, other roosters standing wide-eyed in the yard. Let this be a warning to you! I called—and I held Larry up by the feet to make sure they could see—blood sprinkling on the patio, blood on my hands, blood starting to jelly along the edges of the pan. Began pulling feathers from the bird, feathers off the wings like leaves, soft down underneath like hair, feathers sticking to my hands, garbage bag soon full of feathers, tufts floating like seeds in the light, a chalky taste to swallow away. Followed the directions from a book, chopped off feet, singed hairs with candle, washed bird in ice-cold water, peeled skin from around shoulders, removed crop, removed neck to base, cut away oil gland at tail, scooped insides out of bird—heart, liver, gizzard, all the edible viscera of a fowl good for gravy and stuffing—flushed water all through body, patted skin dry with flour, rubbed with salt and pepper and butter, kept in refrigerator until ready to roast the damned thing.

Nice fresh salad, sweet corn, baked potatoes, table set with candles, napkins in napkin rings, chicken in oven. So domestic—scene straight out of *Better Homes and Gardens*—called my sister in Flushing as I waited for Bob. Wanted to tell Jean my latest chicken adventure. Wanted to tell about the baby

20

kicking field goals into my chest. Wanted to have someone excited for me, hear some echo of my own voice tipping back chipper and happy to me, show myself buoyant as a cork in the world.

She wasn't home from work, most likely—phone ringing, machine picking up—Just wanted to say hello, Jean, thinking of you, will try later. Next came my mother in Greenpoint to dial as I waited for Bob to come home. Still wanted to tell about the baby kicking, the meal I made, the chicken feathers everywhere, give this glimpse of me happy and light to someone, phone ringing and ringing with no one there either. Caught my face in the mirror of the toaster, nose and chin all fun-housed and warped, touched my hair into place, turned away from the counter and sink full of dishes. Bird from the oven, deep breath, and I called the Elks Club, the VFW, the Knights of Columbus.

Sorry, they said, haven't seen him all day—murmur of voices, drone of television, laughter in the background—and I placed the phone in its cradle and waited. Could hear a rooster crowing, but when *couldn't* I hear a rooster crowing? Called the Lions, the Legion Hall, the Elks again. Said, I'd like to leave a message for my husband this time. Thought to try his father, the man telling me he'd not seen him all day, Bob's father asking, Everything all right, kid?

Everything's fine, I said, the baby's kicking is all. Told him this child must like chocolate or ice cream. Told him felt like popcorn going off in me. Told my father-in-law how you'd think there were birds inside me, like little sparrows fluttering in a cage.

He didn't know what to say to any of this—all this girl gush of mine—and I said I'd better let him go now. Was like a movie you've seen how many times—house so quiet you could hear the clock chewing minutes the way an insect chews a leaf—woman sitting at the table alone, candles burning down, faraway sound of cutlery as she eats her ruined dinner, chicken almost impossibly bad, meat both dry as sawdust and tough as butcher's string.

And the rest of the summer? Rest of summer became a countdown of chickens. Rudy, Raphael, Fonzarelli—oven-baked chicken, lemon-ginger chicken with rice, chicken tetrazzini with cream of mushroom soup—poor Earl going into the crockpot as chicken cacciatore with noodles, meat as tough and dry and terrible as all the others. Dreamed raccoons in the coop one night and Oscar and Carlton Fisk were gone the next morning, stray rooster foot under back steps like a gypsy curse. Smelled Randall after a few days under the hood of my Chevelle, bird in the engine where he must have climbed to keep warm one night. Caught Romero inside the house one afternoon, chased him into the bathroom, wrung his neck over the toilet, scratches up and down my arms, needed pliers to pull the pinfeathers out, bird marinating for three and a half days, yet still that bitter tang as we sat down to eat him, meat thick with the taste of metal washers and rubber tubes.

Bob suggested we go to dinner somewhere nice for ourselves. C'mon, he said, before we need a babysitter.

Really tried not to cry in front of him. Still had six roosters and Matilda to go—everything so emotional for me these days—seven months pregnant by now, bone tired all the time, ankles swollen, baby inside with hiccups, baby tossing and turning, baby never still for a moment. And if he—yes, *he,* somehow I just *knew* it was a boy—and if he *did* stop moving, how long before I pushed and poked him back to life again out of fear?

In the meantime, had roosters crowing all hours of the day, neighbors calling with another in their garden, another in their garage, another shitting all up and down their car again, old man Auger phoning to say he'd shoot this goddamn chicken if I didn't march myself over this very minute!

Go ahead! I yelled—my voice more sharp and strained than I hoped—me telling him to save us the trouble and shoot the thing! I'll send another over in the morning! Anything else I can help you with? Or can I go back to my life now?

You used to be such a nice girl, he said. What happened?

Oh, shove it up your ass, I said—and I went outside and glared at the houses on the street, stood defiant as a rooster on the lawn—and then I strutted around to the coop for Matilda, skinny old spinster of a hen. Put her in a box and brought her down to the Farmers' Co-op. Carried her into the store and asked if they could look at a chicken for me. Asked why she might be losing feathers like this. Poultry lice, they said, and showed how to spread her feathers so the powder got all the way to the roots and skin. Asked if lice might be why she never laid any eggs. Try a golf ball, they said, and they dug an old ball from a drawer. Sometimes tricks a hen into starting a clutch, they said. Worth a try at least. Put it in the nesting box with her. And now what else? they asked. What else did I need? Well, I smiled and wondered aloud how to keep roosters off the roof of the house. Piece of rope, they said, and they cut a length of clothesline the size of a snake, telling me to just toss it up there. I laughed at how *easy* life could be—and I paid for the chicken feed and lice powder—and these three wise men walked me to the car, none of them letting me carry a thing in my condition, one with the twenty-five-pound bag of seed, one with the canister of lice-and-mite powder, one with Matilda clucking in her box.

Rode home thinking I should have asked about the bitter taste of Romero. Probably nicked the gallbladder, they'd have told me, smallest touch of bile enough to ruin a whole bird. Should have asked, Why were all the chickens so dry and tough? Probably the way you kill them, they'd have said, all that struggle and stress releasing enzymes, turning the meat stringy and gamy, feathers hard to pull. Should have asked what did *these* men feel when *their* wives were expecting? Did all their worries boil down to money or work or painting the kid's room? Were they afraid to come home for some reason? Did their wives go through town looking for them, wishing their husband's car around every corner, wanting each turn to be the man caulking windows, hoping for them on the sidewalk finishing a cigarette, always a hundred things to do, endless list of errands to run? And did they ever ask their wives along for a little company?

Bob would sometimes ask me along if I found him. He'd clear whatever papers and bottles from the passenger seat, and we'd drop the vacuum at the repair shop, hit the post office and bank, ride to Chepachet to pick up supplies, and maybe stop for lunch along the way. Might start to rain and he could take the rest of the day with me. Couple more chores off the list — return a power drill to Georgie, baby clothes and a crib to pick up from my girlfriend Lydia — and how about a case of beer for his father? Three of us out on the porch, watching the rain come down, Bob and his father going over who'd paid, who hadn't paid, and who had work for them in the next week or two.

Sometimes I'd drive through town and not find him, not see the Impala, not have anywhere to go but home. Awful to just wait for him, just watch the phone on the wall, catch myself listening for the sound of tires in the drive, feel my hopes going all tiptoes toward the door or window, curtains hanging in long breathless folds, daylight lasting forever. Were times I'd get back in the car and still not find him. An hour of looking and past the Elks, the Lions, the Knights of Columbus, and the Impala there at the Legion Hall at last. Car still in the parking lot when I'd check an hour later, still there when he'd call to say he was running late.

And if I said anything?

Well isn't that just perfect? he'd say — and he'd sweep his hand over the living room or dashboard or whatever happened to be in front of him — Bob asking where'd I think this all came from anyway? The house, the car, the jobs, he'd say, the whole operation flows straight from the Elks. It's my job to sit in that place, he'd tell me, his voice thick. I'm on the fucken *clock* when I'm down there, Anna.

I know how hard you work, Bob.

You don't know the first thing about anything, he'd tell

me—and he'd start toward the door—man bouncing the keys in his hand, saying he'd be down at the Legion Hall. Little overtime down at the office, he'd say, if you know what I mean.

Only later would I know what to say to him. In my mind I'd explain how I once pictured ourselves—how I imagined our life as a bridge—nothing as pretty as the Brooklyn Bridge, yet nothing as bad as the Lincoln Tunnel, more the Manhattan Bridge in my dream, two of us some Tinkertoy set of beams and cables lifting from one place, rising high over river, and setting down in a brand-new world.

August, and the baby arrived early. Beautiful little boy, everyone healthy, happy, whole world out in front of us, my mother and sister driving up from the city, flowers and balloons in hospital room, Bob on good behavior with family there, man changing diapers, feeding baby at night, my sister and mother back to Greenpoint in a few days, Bob still good even after everyone had gone, still good after Labor Day, still good without anyone there to watch except his son and me.

Last of the roosters gone, Bob would slip an egg under Matilda every few nights for me to find. Real sweet of him. But like the flowers and ice cream and chocolates he brought home now, I knew it was just sympathy he felt for me.

And when I told him this?

Maybe, he said—though he looked hurt to me—no sly grin on his face, Bob saying he didn't think it was sympathy at all.

September, and I'd be breastfeeding in the middle of the night, entire world asleep except for this beautiful child and me, Bob in the bedroom, his breaths like waves rolling in to shore. October, and checkups for the baby and me still catching myself holding my breath, as if no one deserved to be as happy as this, me whispering to this baby how lucky we were, how lucky we'd been, how lucky we were going to be. November, and everything soft and sunny and Indian-summer warm, and one Saturday afternoon I pulled into the yard to find a surprise of Impala sitting home, Bob on the patio with his friends Domo and Georgie.

Just the way they started toward the car, and then the way they helloed big and loud to me, Bob helping get the baby out of the back seat, Domo and Georgie carrying grocery bags to the house, felt I should be careful of my wallet around them, pocketbook clutched tight under my arm. All right, I said, why you being so nice to me? What d'you want?

Well, actually, said Bob, we were thinking—and at that I saw Matilda on the patio, bird standing under a chair, string tied to her leg—Domo and Georgie grinning when I turned back to them, baby wide-awake in Bob's arms, Bob saying to let him explain.

Seemed Georgie had been bragging how he knew the way to kill chickens, which got Domo incited over this secret recipe of his, which started Bob thinking how he happened to be in possession of a certain hen. And, yes, said Bob, we have been drinking a little.

Okay, I said—and I went over to Matilda—picked her up

and untied her leg and handed her to Georgie. So, I said, let's see who knows how to kill a chicken, and then who knows how to cook it, yes?

One slit behind the ear, according to Georgie, put the bird down on the ground, watch it jump three times, and just like that it'll be dead. Juggler vein, said Georgie—and he touched just behind his own ear—Domo laughing and asking *which* vein was that again?

What, said Georgie, the *juggler* vein.

Jug-u-lar, said Domo, it's called the *jug-u-lar* vein.

That's what I said, asshole, said Georgie—and everyone laughed, even the baby in Bob's arms smiled, Bob and I saying that was what Georgie said—Domo calling us all dumbass crazy as he went to start the grill. Meanwhile, Georgie held the bird, said a little prayer, cut just behind her ear, and set her down on the ground. Damned if she didn't jump three times and keel over dead on the grass.

Men all looked over to me—not to worry, I smiled, no pangs from this farm girl—Georgie starting to pluck and clean the bird, feathers melting away at his touch, giblets in one dish for gravy, bird washed and cleaned and ready before we even knew.

Domo sprinkled rosemary on the chicken, salt and pepper, garlic powder, and took a can of beer from the cooler at our feet. Opened the beer and made a joke out of putting the can inside the bird. Excuse my reach, he coughed. Sorry, old girl, pardon me now.

Waste of a perfectly good beer if you ask me, said Georgie.

But no one *asked* you, said Domo—and he stood the bird on the grill and closed the lid—and Bob wondered who was thirsty. Passed ice-wet cans of beer from the cooler, sun dappling through the trees, air pouring cool and clean over the yard. We drank our beer, bundled the baby against the dusk, and ate the chicken. It tasted delicious. We wiped our plates with pieces of bread.

Later that night I dreamed a rooster into the yard—some prodigal bird starting to crow from the roof of the garage—and I woke to the sound of a baby crying. How lonely and faraway it sounded. I hoped this child had someone to take care of it, a mother to see if everything was all right, a father to lift it from the crib, check its diaper, pat it quiet on the back. Felt my milk let down—that sweet draw of ache from deep inside—and I started toward the baby's room and heard Bob's voice from the dark.

It's okay, little guy, he was saying. Just woke up funny. Had a bad dream is all. There, there, there, there, there.

THE GHOSTWRITER

And the Lord says, *Go to Peoria.*

Give away all you possess, and go.

If you desire to do my will, if you wish to be my servants, then I have a place for you there.

Now stop—just stop for a moment and feel that voice—*Go to Peoria.*

Imagine being told to give up your present life, give away everything, and follow this command. God's just come to you, told you exactly what to do with your life, and now what? What kind of choice would you have? Scared to obey, scared not to obey, and then there's your family, your friends, your mother-in-law, your neighbors. You have to break the news to them all. Have to quit your jobs, turn off the gas and electric, stop the mail, shut off the phone. Have to pull the kids out of school. Have to pack up a van and say goodbye to everything and everyone you've ever known.

You barely know where Peoria is, but God's been pretty

clear and direct on this. You find yourself driving a van all day and night until you reach, at long last, Illinois. Couple more hours and you're on the outskirts—Peoria—next six exits. The city line, and you pull over to the side of the highway, traffic rushing past, fields lying flat with dirty snow.

I'm the ghostwriter who spends all morning with this man. I listen as he calmly tells how he and his family sat there with day fading to night, lights of the city in the distance, his wife and three kids shivering in the cold. All five of them wait and pray on the shoulder of the highway. God had directed them only as far as Peoria, so they didn't know what to do except wait for His next directive. And, yes, it all sounds completely crazy to him too, he says, which makes me like this man. He knows this is all beyond reason. No one could understand it, he tells me, none of it rational, the way he received word from God, the way God was so specific, the way they unloaded everything they owned, the way they followed this voice to Illinois.

The story was sent to the magazine where I work, a religious-minded monthly where my job is to rewrite these true stories of hope and inspiration. We're not sold on newsstands, but we have almost four million subscribers and have been rolling out our brand of good news to the world for more than fifty years—first-person accounts, taken from actual events, all of which serve as testaments of faith of some sort—or as the magazine's mission statement says, our articles present time-tested methods for developing courage, strength, and positive attitudes through faith.

My job is to make sure that the piece conforms to the expectations of our readers. In short, each story needs its all-walks-of-life beginning, its crisis of faith, its turnaround and ultimate triumph of spirit, its upswing of happy and positive and purpose-to-it-all ending. I make all the narratives fit this template and shepherd the authors through the process, so that they sign off on the pieces, attesting that everything is real and true and completely their own.

All stories must be personal experiences of God's goodness—whatever that may mean—and this goodness must shine through somehow in the unfolding events. In-house, we call this "God factor" in a story its *cello*, as in the musical instrument. And when line edits come back to us, we ghostwriters get suggestions like *more cello* or *less cello* or *where's the cello?*

Every aspect of our job is meant to serve the cello, and the cello is supposed to build to the story's ultimate payoff: that bright-lit moment when we understand that everything has worked out, that the family has found a home in Peoria, that their home was wherever God wanted them to be.

The stories I'm assigned run the gamut. A guy rescues manatees in Florida. A crop-duster or beekeeper or fisherman survives some great accident or addiction or loss. Someone finds an unopened letter from World War II and forwards it to the widow. The variations are endless for us line-workers at the epiphany plant, the meaning of life packaged into nice, tidy, fifteen-hundred-word servings of conflict, crisis, and radiant revelation.

We crank them out like widgets—these little air pockets

of cello—no story complete without its takeaway. In the epiphany business, each takeaway must be as short and sweet and hopeful as possible. In the jargon of the office, the classic stories boil down to some variation of *IPIG*—I Prayed I Got—or *ITIJ*—I Trust in Jesus (and that's made all the difference).

Truth is, my days are fabulous, literally alive with people who talk to God—help this, rescue that, thank you for these, may I please have those—the typical silence of God becoming a kind of Rorschach test for the protagonists. My narrators usually fill this silence with the needs or fears or desires of their lives and circumstances. What makes the Peoria story so fascinating to me is that God not only spoke to these people, but He did so in such a specific and puckish way.

I love the image of them on the side of the highway, can feel the tug of trucks rushing past, can see the guardrails, the stray muffler, the shreds of tire, the man and his family stranded on Interstate 74, all of them wondering what to do, where to go, how to continue. They're cold and hungry and afraid. It's quiet and getting dark. The cars, the trucks, the darkness, and they wait for as long as they can, but nothing happens.

It's the middle of the week and they drive to the first motel they find. All five of them in a grubby little room. Two, three, four days passing. Five days of praying and watching television. Sunday morning, down to their last twelve dollars, they check out of the motel and go a few blocks to the nearest church. They are the only black family in all the pews, the columns and windows and tall space of the church around them, the last of their money going into the collection plate, their last possession released. And here they are—those first quiet chords of cello—because at the end of the sermon, as everyone files out of the church, the pastor stands on the front steps to greet the parishioners, to receive these new visitors, thank them for attending the service, small talk about the weather and the sermon and the church, cello rising as he asks where's home for them, anyway?

We came from New York, they tell him, but we have nowhere to go. The Lord told us to come to Peoria, that he would give us a place here, and we found your church.

The pastor calls everyone back to the steps, his voice lifting over the cello, the man announcing that *this* was the family they'd been expecting, *these* were the people they'd been told to prepare for. And by the end of the day—whole string section of cellos and violins and violas by now—soundtrack soaring as this family finds a home in Peoria, a set of jobs, a new school, furnishings and clothing and food and everything they need, this little parish waiting for their arrival all along.

It's a crazy, miracle-laden story, which barely makes any sense. Yet talking to this man, I see he's not the unquestioning fanatic I first imagined. In fact, by the middle of our conversation—which ranges from the poetry of Walt Whitman to the grace of rivers and trees to why pride is the last possession we seem able to release—and I know that something extraordinary has happened to this man. I'm almost envious as I jot the details, the role of faith in his life, that echo of God's voice in his words. It's easy to obey and serve the Lord when you have security, he says to me. It's quite easy when your insurance and rent are paid. But try giving away everything, putting yourself at stake for something in the world, because *that* is where faith and trust and believing begin.

And as I copy my shorthand notes, as I line up the elements of his story, I'm more and more convinced that he made this cold-sweat leap, that he trusted himself to something greater than himself, that he had his doubts every step of the way, and that, as a result of this test, he has touched some deep and profound belief. Whether you call this religious or not, you can't go through an experience like this without something spiritual happening to you.

I edge a photograph of the man and his family onto my computer screen—all of them smiling and dressed in royal-blue choir gowns—and just the *idea* of them in Peoria seems enough to fill me with a sense of hope and well-being. I feel like a tuning fork as I work on the story of the man and his family, the faint hum of my own commandments coming to life in the calm tone of the man's voice.

Later that week, when I turn in my draft, I am high on the piece. I go office to office, saying good night to everyone. I ride the elevator down to New York City and find myself outside, walking in the twilight and the passing crowds and steam of midtown, the braying car horns and burning smell of rubber and pretzel salt. I'm on my way home to Brooklyn with this feeling, this glimmer of what it's like when *what you believe* and *what you do* are one and the same thing.

I am flying—*cello, don't fail me now*—and am part of the
well-join'd scheme that Whitman always sings about, myself
disintegrated, everyone disintegrated, all of us disintegrated
yet part of the scheme:

Just as you feel when you look on the river and sky, so I felt,
Just as any of you is one of a living crowd, I was one of a
crowd,
Just as you are refresh'd by the gladness of the river and the
bright flow, I was refresh'd,
Just as you stand and lean on the rail, yet hurry with the
swift current, I stood, yet was hurried . . .

And all I can say is yes.
To the whole wheeling world, I'm saying, Yes.
Yes, yes, yes, and yes.
And when I get the story back for revision the next morn-
ing, my editor has written over that cello-soaked takeaway of
mine:

PREACH IT, BROTHER BILLY!!!
PREACH IT!!!

And the truth? The truth is that I hear commandments as
well—vague and small-voiced—and I believe, for better or
worse, everyone else hears them too. And what, in the end,
is the difference between *Go to Peoria* and *Write the book?* Or
Marry the girl? Or any of the countless passions that guide our
days? Who are we, truly, if not these dreams, these pursuits,

these acts of faith? What are we but these urges? What else carries us through our lives, gives us meaning, helps us make sense of the accidents that befall us? And when I think of it like this, I actually *feel* — or *believe* — that the best in us is utterly mad. The meaning of our lives, our purpose, everything we care about starts as a dim voice, a small urge driving us on to our own kinds of Peoria.

I feel like a whistleblower telling you all of this, spilling the inner workings of the ghostwriter, the daily life of the anonymous content provider, humble commodifier of insight and faith. The less flattering side, of course, is that I milk a good week and a half out of the Peoria story, revise it a few times at my leisure, and then it's gone from my life.

The next ditty arrives on my desk, another wave on the shore, roughly two or three per issue. This week astronaut lady, next week Iwo Jima guy, someone always climbing a mountain or surviving a flood or shipwreck or farm accident — these are the bread-and-butter events of God — and we line-workers rarely do justice to the stories that deserve it, just as we do too much justice to the stories that don't.

Still, there are worse ways to make a living. I spend my days learning about manatees and listening to people who live with angels and other spirits. I have an editor who saves the most interesting assignments for me, who teaches me to care about things, who helps make my work the best it can be. What more could I ask? I mean, he only needs to gooseline a word or write in the margin *WCDB* — We Can Do Better — and I understand exactly what he sees and needs. I have a place in the world and sit in editorial meetings and read from the hundreds of prayers that arrive every week, my colleagues passing snapshots of clouds or trees that resemble Moses or Mother Teresa, the likeness often uncanny, the letters and newspaper clippings never ending.

How humbling to consider all the boxes of mail, year after year, all these cards and stories arriving, and then to think of all the stories *not* written and *not* sent? What about all the families that must pass unnoticed for every Peoria, all the dim urges that never quite work out in our lives, and then, by extension, all those cruel and vengeful and unspeakable hungers of ours, those terrible impulses that we can neither resist nor understand?

Again, Uncle Walt, talk to me:

> *It is not upon you alone the dark patches fall,*
> *The dark threw its patches down upon me also,*
> *The best I had done seem'd to me blank and suspicious,*
> *My great thoughts as I supposed them, were they*
>   *not in reality meagre?*
> *Nor is it you alone who know what it is to be evil,*
> *I too knitted the old knot of contrariety,*
> *Blabb'd, blush'd, resented, lied, stole, grudg'd,*
> *Had guile, anger, lust, hot wishes I dared not speak,*
> *Was wayward, vain, greedy, shallow, sly, cowardly,*
>   *malignant,*
> *The wolf, the snake, the hog, not wanting in me,*

The cheating look, the frivolous word, the adulterous
wish, not wanting,
Refusals, hates, postponements, meanness, laziness,
none of these wanting,
Was one with the rest, the days and haps of the rest . . .

I keep Whitman at my desk like a pint of whiskey — the
wolf, the snake, the hog, not wanting in me either — and I
stare out my window at the city, the sky, the buildings like so
many piles of nickels and pennies in the light. Sun going down,
people going home, and I too have been living the same life
with the rest, the same old laughing, gnawing, sleeping . . .

Play'd the part that still looks back on the actor or actress,
The same old role, the role that is what we make it, as
great as we like,
Or as small as we like, or both great and small.

After Whitman, I study Emerson for a puff piece about a
house where he once stayed, which is now a bed-and-break-
fast. I read all about Emerson for days — Knight of Grief, Pa-
tron Saint of Self-Reliance — and I keep coming back to the
moment when he opens the coffin of his wife. Little more than
a year since her death, and there's Emerson, walking to the
cemetery, standing in the cool of the tomb, lifting the lid of
the box with a need to prove what? That it's all not just some
dream? That she is dead and gone and will never answer the
letters he continues to write to her in his journals? *That*, in his

words, *though the wide universe is full of good, no kernel of nourishing corn can come to him but through his toil bestowed on that plot of ground which is given to him to till?*

I am already two or three stories away from Peoria by the time the galleys come back to me, the page proofs sitting on my chair when I arrive at work one morning. We aren't allowed major edits at this point in the issue—nothing that will change the formatting or layout of the page—only the stray typo to catch, the inevitable wince of overwriting, the awkward phrase, all the missteps that bump you out of the narrative spell.

There's no reason to call, no unfinished business about this story, yet I can't help but phone the church pastor in Peoria under the pretext of fact checking. I want to hear again what happened, how the family appeared in his pews one day, how the congregation had been waiting for them, how there was a house sitting ready, walls freshly painted only a few days before. I ask for details about life in Peoria, about the mills, the layoffs at Caterpillar, the heavy trains of the Central Illinois pounding through at night, all the little proofs that lead up to this family just arriving.

They came to us from nowhere, he tells me again, his voice quiet and calm and patient. Was just a miracle, he says, really, and I can't explain any of it to you.

THE ARCHITECT OF FLOWERS

I.

Sometimes a single flower, a single petal on the ground, and she'd go all shattery. A bird trapped in the greenhouse and she'd be unable to move, knees trembling against the front of her skirt, the old woman expecting always to find the man dead in the orchard, or dead in the gardens, or dead in the crawlspace under the begonias, where he kept a cot and some grubbing tools. It was a fear she'd held so long she'd begun to secretly crave it—the hybridizer slumped over his seed-beds at last—part of her flustered and hurrying out through ferns and palms to him, part of her dawdling over zinnias and hoyas, lingering under this déjà vu of leaves and trees, wandering as if his death was just some long-standing social effort before her, the ballet or the dentist, just some dread dinner engagement she hoped to slip completely.

And a fear, she knew, a fear must be a secret kind of wish, a seed from which some fruit must follow. Her husband gone, the greenhouses gone, the flowers all scattered to the wind. She longed for these things to fall like truncheons on her body, yearned for the worst to simply happen, her heart going like a bird in her chest at times. And not a small bird either, her heart like a pigeon or a crow, its wings trying to open inside the cage of her ribs. She'd try to steady herself against this rush of feeling, hold a stack of clay pots or a wooden trellis of ivy until the moment passed, her skin like velvet brushing one way, her skin like velvet brushing the other. Back and forth like this until she gradually came to herself once more, the old woman lost again in these fragile houses of glass, lost among the flowers of the gift shop, her shop with its packets of seeds, its tins of grafting wax, its watering cans, trowels, and fancy hand-carved dibbers.

And for such a small shop on an old post road away from town, the bells on the door never seemed to stop ringing. The whole room would be caught off guard, and she'd turn each time to the open door, her eyes first hopeful, then crestfallen, as if he might have surprised her just this once, some new consolation of flowers in his hands. She'd recover quickly enough—as practiced in her disappointments as she was—yet who could miss that sad air of regret in the room? The way she hiked the smile back onto her face?

Students, tourists, garden societies from the valley, but never her husband, never her son, never anyone she truly wanted to see in the doorway. Forever just the mailman, the beekeeper, the auctioneer with that little dog in his arms. A kiss to one cheek, a kiss to the other, and the auctioneer would set his dog on the floor and assume a cup of tea, a wedge of lemon, and a tiny silver spoon, which he'd stir and keep stirring.

Seemed endless, spoon back and forth in the teacup, the auctioneer browsing whatever houseplants and clutter she had for sale, his little dog tottering about the aisles, its leg lifting to magazines and books piled near the wall. Always left her speechless, that scrabble of the animal's toenails over the wood of the floor, the auctioneer standing cool and nonchalant as he set the spoon on the counter in front of her just so, the man so offhanded and casual as he priced a pair of lamps, an antique harrowing rake, an old farmer's sink invaluable to certain collectors in the city, all the things he could sell for her. The auctioneer talked so calm, so matter-of-fact, he made her nightmares seem ridiculous to her, which made her nightmares somehow worse.

A sip of tea and he'd ask about the greenhouses, the orchards, the seed stock, all of his questions so perfectly reasonable that they made her wince at herself. What would happen to the gardens when the hybridizer was gone? What would become of the flowers? And then what would become of her? What did her son say? What did her husband say? What did she say about all of this?

She never lied to him—unless silence was a kind of lie—but she did have a way of turning such questions into answers all their own. A glance, a finger to her lips, and she steered the auctioneer around to pruning shears and a new batch of lilies, and how about a pinch of caramel ivy for him to taste? Here, she said, and smiled. Take some rose-hip jelly for your mother.

She patienced him out onto the porch, the auctioneer calling zoom-zoom for his little dog. And what a relief as he drove away finally, his car cresting the hill, the woman feeling she'd just survived another brush with death, her body full of birds once more, sparrows this time, hundreds of them, her lips pressed tight against the din. A deep breath and she would turn back to her husband, the hybridizer out in the orchard or potting shed or forcing house.

II.

He came from a long line of flower makers and was prolific and lucky and could bring almost any scent or color to life. There was once a rose of chocolate that he made for her, its buds like little fruit moths all powdered with cocoa. There were asters and orchids and clover that he invented, a foxglove for her birthday, a candied basil for their son. He sometimes stumbled across those forgotten heirlooms in the woods—a tiny iris in the weeds of an old cemetery, a patch of gardenia in a field of unmown hay—and even the old hybridizer would begin to wonder if they'd only dreamed the flowers.

He'd be working in the greenhouse or the garden, transplanting hoyas or sweetpeas, and he could sense his wife's approach in the leaves around him, the stems and branches tightening like the cordage on a ship before a storm. He'd be right in front of her—the hybridizer alive and well as ever—up to his elbows in bedding plants when she found him, that crooked smile on his face.

Oh, shush yourself, she'd say—and he'd not have said a word, of course—his wife starting in about star-nosed moles in the orchard, about the auctioneer with his little dog, about the caladiums going all to hell right here under his very nose. Didn't they look a little leggy to him? Maybe hold off water a couple days to harden them up? Maybe some cow's milk?

He watched as she busied herself with cyclamen and gardenia, pinched off stems and flowers, the woman cleaning the marigolds to within an inch of their lives, the hybridizer smiling at the way she'd glance every so often to him, as if she was genuinely irritated to find him here.

Now don't start with me, she told him—and he laughed out loud to her—his wife brushing her hands clean, wiping her nose, and mussing the leaves of the caladiums once again. The hybridizer enjoyed the way she'd flit over the plants like this, her eyes and face and voice her own again, the woman telling about the day's mail, the local weather reports, her afternoon at the shop.

You know, she said, I could use a little nice from you.

Just a little?

A little would be a start, wouldn't it?

He laughed and she shooed him from the greenhouse toward the rest of his day. Had errands to run, didn't he? Caraway and fennel to the village bistro, aloe to the glassman, and if he so much as glanced back to the house, he knew she would be standing on the side of the road, her arms raised for him to keep it moving, the old woman watching until he disappeared down the hill.

As he walked, he didn't mean to become like his wife about such things, but the hybridizer swore he could hear

47

her huff herself back into the house. Was a trick of cathedrals—that faint sound of cutlery and dishes carrying from the kitchen—the woman telling the cupboards how unappreciated she was around here, how the man couldn't build the first weed without her. Be like going without sunlight or soil or whatever else his stupid flowers seemed to need. Like selfishness, apparently. Must take great gobs of selfishness to make the ugliest little plant. Selfishness, obstinacy, and who knows what else? Sure can't hurt to live like a hermit, it looks like. And to be uncivil and short-tempered and flatulent and—oh, yes—have I mentioned selfishness yet? Selfishness, pishy-pash, and complete utter madness, that great trinity of flower making—more important than seeds or sun or rain or the mystery of a good goddamn wife! Ha!

Fresh flowers to bring to the church, eucalyptus and poppies to the apothecary, it all seemed normal enough, little scraps of gossip swirling endlessly after him as he breezed into town—a geranium said to be more venomous than a snake, his wife rumored to poison the man every evening, their son known to have escaped like bittersweet from the gardens—and the hybridizer with his usual stops to the blacksmith, the stationer, the glassworks.

Behind the glassyard walls lay piles of sand and lime and soda ash, dusty stacks of glassware and bottles on wooden pallets, mounds of scrap glass broken into cullet to be stirred back into the crucible again. The glassman and his son worked in the pit as if in deep water, everything slow and highly keyed, and the hybridizer stared down at the matching whorls of hair, the long swan's neck of a pitcher coming to life at the end of the gaffer's tube. And as the glassman's son carried the pitcher to the annealing ovens, the old glassman set aside the trimming tools, the light going murky as they dampened the kilns, the young man returning with a wineskin of water for his father, the glassman tipping it up like a trumpet, and there he was, that old scarecrow of a man, the hybridizer smiling down at them from the rail. The hybridizer shook his head in mock disapproval, as if they'd played the whole father-son scene a bit too neat, a tad too tidy for his taste, the glassman hollering something over the din of fans, something hunger, something thirst, his throat dry and sore and ruined by kilns.

Out in the sun and the two men walked past the lumberyards and brickworks, that taste of river in the air as they reached the canal, the water all chromed and curdled with oil and sewage. At the tavern they could talk philodendrons and tapered stemware and whatever else occupied their minds—be it wives or work or money or children—both men had grown up in the valley and taken the trades of their fathers. The glassman's father made his name in petticoat insulators for the railroad and telegraph, while the hybridizer's father led an almost monastic life of seeds and soil, his own father, the hybridizer's grandfather, once holding the patent to a variation of peppermint (*Mentha piperita*), which he made by crossing watermint (*Mentha aquatica*) and spearmint (*Mentha spicata*).

And in the back garden of the tavern, the hybridizer and the glassman could eat and drink, each of them able to glance at the other and catch himself in the mirror of his friend. That same gathering of tired under the eyes and chin, the overripe ears and nose, hair all gone to seed, hands either smooth and scarred from fire and glass or else stained by soil and thickened from roots. In either case, one need only look across the table to see that time was not some vague abstraction after all, not some idea in which to believe or not to believe. Time had become, instead, the last great theme of life. And the cliché of it only made things worse, the hybridizer sitting with his glass of port, his hands having turned into gloves, all knotted and spotted and strange, his real fingers and palms still somehow soft and clean and unspoiled inside.

Sunlight through the trees, a truck horn, a faint howl of the train in the distance, all evidence that life would go on without them, that it went along just fine without them already. Birds chittering in the leaves, an airplane across the sky, and the waitress made her rounds of coffee and finger cakes, and they ordered one more round of port, why not?

A breeze passed over the garden, the air moving like a school of fish through the ivy and the trees. And it might have been the port talking, but the hybridizer edged forward in his chair and said he had some bad news. It would appear, he said, that she thinks I'm about to die again.

The glassman leaned toward his friend—he'd been facing the hybridizer all along, but he seemed to face him even more somehow—Always good to know these things, he said. And how, may I ask, are you supposed to take your leave of us *this* time?

She didn't say exactly, said the hybridizer. Though it must be soon, my demise, judging by the way she's acting.

The glassman affected a priestly manner, pressed his hands around the glass of port. I have to say, he said, you've certainly *looked* better.

Thanks, friend.

Any time, said the glassman — and he finished his port and signaled the waitress for the check — and he waited and turned the empty glass on the napkin as if to focus something.

The hybridizer hummed, church bells tolling in the distance, the hybridizer pointing to the sound. See? he said. The real problem is she's just going to be *right* one of these days.

Damn woman, said the glassman. Like a broken clock, isn't she?

III.

A gust of birds across the yard, the dull ache of rain approaching in her knuckles, and she turned to the house again. A crow cawed from far away, and the hybridizer's wife lifted her face to the sun and took a deep breath. Enough is enough, old woman. She scolded herself back toward the iron gate, the front walk — such a fine porch, such a handsome rhododendron — and she felt like a guest arriving to the party early. Nothing quite ready yet. No one quite here. A pair of pigskin gloves on the steps, and that long momentum of sadness as she taunted herself back into the kitchen.

Not anything too subtle about the phone in front of her. A call to the city would make it real. Just that grainy hello of her son in the long distance, the distracted way he had of answering — his voice so busy, so brusque — if anything could bring her back to herself, if anything could put her back down in the world, it was her son so clear and far away on the phone like this. She went all bristles and tin metal, little birds in the cage of her body again, her finger ready on the cradle as her son said hello.

I'm sorry, she said. I didn't catch you at a bad time, did I?

A slight hitch in the connection and she heard him swallow liquid on the other end of the line. It's not a bad time, he was telling her, but I can't just sit and chat right now, either, Mom.

I'll let you go, she said, her voice strong and breezy and so obviously hurt. She didn't mean to go all martyr on him, didn't want to be so heavy and difficult, her son trying to ask if everything was all right.

Oh, everything's just fine, she told him — and she watched her feelings catch up to her — felt like a coin was rolling down the slot, wheel tipping some mechanism into motion, this unexpected prize suddenly there in her mouth. Everything's just fine, she said. Except your father, of course, he's just died in the greenhouse.

IV.

One could make a holiday out of such a passage. Overnight on a train, steady ticker tape of wheels on rails, city devolving into suburbs and farms, and a young man able to find a compartment to himself, able to slowly acclimate himself from one world and life to another. Back in the city he worked in buttons. Glass buttons, plastic buttons, buttons of silver, copper, brass, coral, leather, lacquer, amber, pewter, gold. Buttons of broken china. Buttons of shipwrecked coins. Five, seven, eleven years in buttons and beads and able to recite the breathless rise of the lowly button in his sleep, its under-dog days as hopeless decoration, early alliance with suspender and belt, marriage to buttonhole, love affairs with safety pin and clasp hook, mentor to the metal snap, arch-nemesis of the zipper.

And for filling his head with such nonsense he was what, again, please? Well compensated? A company man on the rise? Stray buttons clattering to the floor when he took off his clothes at night? Buttons in bed with him when he woke in the morning? And didn't life just love its little ironies, its little cir-cles and inside jokes, like the one about a certain son of a cer-tain botanist who was fated to—of all things—a life of but-tons, even the word itself coming from the French *bouton,* as in *bud,* literally, *of a flower?*

Surely it's true, no one sets out to make his head a piggy bank full of buttons, just as no one dreams of becoming the type of man who feels only what when his father dies? In-convenienced? Annoyed when his mother calls to fetch him home? What kind of son hopes, even briefly, that his own mother would just slip away in her sleep? Who wishes to be done with the entire chore of them, his parents just another task of many tasks on a list?

His temple to the train's cool rattle of glass, that swal-low's flight of wires at the window, and it was his share of the greenhouses that he sat there calculating. The gardens, the seed stock, the old farmhouse to expedite. The value of the hill to developers, the woods to lumber interests, furniture to the auctioneer, and not even the slightest groan of shame rose out of him. Not even a seedling of loss or sadness or anything. He began to wonder if a lack of feeling was a feeling. And he worried that it was.

He might not have wanted to become his father—endless taste of fertilizer in the back of his throat, burn of pesticide in the cuts on his hands, world as small and close as a greenhouse—but at least the old man never sat at a desk counting out buttons like so many nickels and dimes. At least his father hadn't lived his life by aversion, hadn't moved always away from what he didn't want, the old hybridizer not afraid to go toward things, to hope for things, to dream of things. At least his father's life had been pulled by sunlight, relieved by rain, urged by roots and leaves. Each daffodil, each tulip, every pane of glass in the greenhouse such a matter of life or death to the old hybridizer. At least his father cared about things and kept caring about them, the man caring so much that he didn't care if anyone else cared, which seemed to make people care, students and tourists and garden societies from the valley practically swooning their way up the hill to the greenhouses and gardens and gift shop, that jangle of bells on the door always ringing. At least the old man and his wife hadn't spent their days just hoping to feel, hadn't kept wishing their lives would just begin, hadn't wasted their nights just yearning to yearn for something.

The train ran as smooth as a trance, and the hybridizer's son opened the window and stood and held his face to the wind. He closed his eyes to the gathering speed of wheels on rails under him. And maybe it was the smell of fields, or the feel of rain, or the damp cool of night—maybe it was the tree-softened hills in the distance, or that long call of the engine's whistle from far ahead—but then maybe it was his father, finally, that urge of seedlings that the hybridizer's son could feel in his throat. Felt like a tulip bulb in the notch of his neck, crocus corms fingering their way out of him, that first surge of sadness and he was almost happy, the hybridizer's son almost relieved, as if all he'd needed was a seed to nurture, the littlest seed able to wedge the strongest stone in two.

And just as this long cry was rising out of him, the door of the compartment clanged open. He jumped back at the noise, a young couple in the brightness of the hall. Sorry, they said—the girl with her pretty laughter—the two of them running and giggling all the way down the corridor to the vestibule at the end of the car. So many ways to go through this life, he thought to himself, wondering what did he really want? And what was he so afraid of?

He pushed the window closed and sat as the train ran smooth and effortless again, the stillness of movement, night passing without seeming to pass at all. And in this séance of trees and moon he all but saw them, a boy and his father waist-deep in deer brush and empty mill yards. The man could startle flowers from a field in the way other men might start rabbits. He'd summon each plant by name—red button-straw, wild knotweed—the old hybridizer calling flowers to his hand as if calling songbirds, as good as creating every trait of leaf and root by simply handing it to his son. Take the lance-leafed wood fern, its scent of sun-warm hayfields, its leaves closing as if to sleep at night. Take an old mountain ash in the middle of the woods, symbol of grandeur, leaves said to cure warts and rickets, bark a source of blue for dyers, seeds used in spells requiring focus and strength of purpose. Take a stone wall and the double life of lichen—half fungus, half algae—a symbiosis one could rub into dust with one's fingers.

And home in the gardens, take the old hybridizer and his wife, companion plants of a kind to each other, carrots thriving next to onions, asparagus next to parsley. Once found them lying naked in the garden together, the boy looking and looking until he knew what he was seeing, their skin glowing against the soil, his mother's clothes draped over the rose hedge. Have they just made love? Are they really just testing the dirt, as they said, just seeing if the soil is comfortable for seeds? They expected him to believe that? His mother the color of boiled potatoes? His father's penis hanging like a nose?

No wonder he couldn't help but stare.

No wonder he couldn't help but look away.

No wonder he felt so many different things at the same time.

Above the seat was a reading lamp. Even here he didn't read so much as weigh the letters in his hands, pieces of mail from his father, props in case he was called upon to say a few words at the service.

His mother would be seeing to all the arrangements. The church, the cemetery, she'd be the widow at the door, her dress so blue it would practically shimmer with despair, that splash of baby's breath at her collar for life would go on. Everyone would be so hushed and sincere, the hybridizer lying in the parlor, surrounded by flowers.

A confetti of pressed ferns from one letter. A line about an early snow from another. A delivery of bees. A quick note on Mendel's Third Law of Dominance and Progressive Heredity. A postscript, his father's hand like the tracks of insects:

> I don't know about people, but I've found periods of great changefulness alternate with periods of stability and relative stasis in plants. They seem to leap as well as creep, and novel characters suddenly appear in great perfection, not linked to their parents in any halfway stages. (No doubt a scrap of hope for offspring everywhere!)

And from the next a sprig of damselweed and his father's voice he could hear as he read:

> Thank you for the wonderful weekend, which your mother and I enjoy more each time we remember it to one another. Turned out we waited quite a while at the station after you left. Mechanical trouble, apparently, had to get a new locomotive. Almost called you at work, but a man, a stranger, took us to lunch and told us about the history of this and that place nearby. And in spite of our being so late, it was pure glory when we settled ourselves and got going at long last. A few hours from home and there was another delay. In any case, we kept losing time, the countryside creeping along the final hours, our minds fixed firmly on home. All of which made us feel how you and the city were quite remote to us, remote like the moon.

Was only the speed of the train in all likelihood, but the letter trembled in his hand. He remembered leaving them at the station that morning, his parents as delicate as ash, everything shades of gray, concrete, steam, steel, sky. They looked so bewildered and lost to him in the city, grins frozen dumb on their faces, same as in the elevator to his office, same as at the alumni club, with his button colleagues joking about Velcro and toggle loops. And in the taxi cab that night, the lights of the streets slurred with rain, and he could still feel his mother as tight as a bird next to him, her fingers strong as talons on his arm.

Even his mother — he could practically see her — the hybridizer's wife becoming her devotions, the woman as good as being those fragile houses of glass. And he remembered being this skinny little kid among the hundred-year-old olive and fig trees, leaves and branches bent flush to the slanted roof of glass, the trunks like cables tied to the ground. He remembered how he'd somehow gotten it into his head that he could cut them all free with the claw end of a hammer, the boy chopping at the trees so that the greenhouses could float gently away.

For miles he rode like this, a wide black shine of lake swinging into view, a stadium of trees, clouds all snowcapped with moon. The conductor called down the corridor as they approached the next station, scrap yards and factories and lights, the squall of crossing bells, passengers and hawkers on the platform, peanuts and pillows for sale, heavy thumps of baggage, mailbags, that pigeon-murmur of loudspeakers, and then forward again, everything as gradual as a ship under sail.

The car rocked as they picked up speed—and the door to the compartment opened—an older gentleman standing in the light. He apologized for the intrusion, but asked was that seat free by any chance? Not riding terribly far, he said, if that was any consolation.

The hybridizer's son moved his things out of the way, the old man sat with a suitcase between his feet, trees flocking close to the windows, pines like crows at the glass, the old man straightening his jacket, loosening his collar and tie. The train ran fast and straight and smooth over darkened fields, and the old man asked, Are you inclined to speak with people on trains?

I'm sorry?

I usually like to ask, said the man, as some do find it a burden to make the effort. A condition I completely understand, if you'd rather keep to yourself.

No-no, said the hybridizer's son—and he straightened up in his seat—saying he'd just been thinking a little company would be nice.

The old man smiled and soon told how he was a doctor in a previous life. Small-town practice, he said, mostly babies and broken bones. Wife passed a few years ago. Son lives in the next town. Daughter lives in the city. Precious little else attaching him to the world any longer, just some far-flung grandchildren here and there.

The two of them watched the trees gather outside, a loud branch against the side of the car startling them, both of them smiling to each other. The train in deep timber for what turned out to be miles, the doctor saying how he loved to travel like this. And so, he said, what puts a young man on a train in the middle of the week these days, anyway? Love or money?

Probably both, said the hybridizer's son. My father died today—or died yesterday by now—and my mother called and I got on a train.

The old man hummed slightly, but he didn't say how sorry he was, didn't ask how close they were, didn't try to fill the compartment with chatter. Instead the old doctor just sat still and quiet, his face almost granular in the light, as if his skin was made of marzipan. And there it was again, that strange surge of sadness in his throat, the hybridizer's son trying to swallow it away. And when the old man asked what he did in the world, the hybridizer's son said that he made flowers.

And because the lie seemed so true all of a sudden—so true and necessary to him—the hybridizer's son leaned forward and said it again. I make flowers, he told the man. Flowers and vegetables, he said, and he continued to tell what he suddenly most wanted to hear. I listen to plants all day, he said. Which means I care about soil and sunlight and seasons and seeds and dew points. I walk through roses as if they were rooms in my mind. I lie awake at night with the problems of Mendel's peas and what turns them white and what turns them back to pink. I smell like fertilizer and grafting wax. I always have dirt on my hands.

And your father did the same?

He did.

And your mother?

Of course.

And your wife and children?

Yes, said the hybridizer's son, I'm lucky that way.

V.

There once was a language of flowers. A handful of hawthorn for a safe journey home. Hyacinth for forgiveness. Ferns making everything sincere. And if she dawdled over zinnia this time—flower of maternal love—it was because each orange petal put her son on a train to her. A lifetime of lingering, but at least now it was hope—daisies and bluebells—that drew her through the rooms of the house, at least now it was some promise of happiness—crocus and dahlia—that pulled her up the stairs to her son's room.

She stood in the doorway—her husband's boyhood room, as well, come to think of it—same windows, same narrow bed, same angle of roofline in the ceiling. And she could close her eyes and follow the train along the stitches of track in her mind, the map all watercolor blues of rivers and lakes, tans and browns of mountains, cities marked with circles, towns with stars. The speed would gutter like a candle at his window. Trees would pass, all feathered and silver with night. Nothing she couldn't imagine about his arrival home. Are you hungry? she'd ask. How was your trip? Should we go find your father?

She pushed herself from the doorway and drifted down the hall to their bedroom, where she hovered over the old man's dresser, the nursery catalogues, the papers, a bobby pin he stole from her to clean his ears. There were crows outside in the orchard—might have been bickering for hours, but she heard them back and forth now—and she let herself sit on her husband's side of the bed. She lay back into that old sag of his body, that smell of fish emulsion in his pillow, that tang of his hair. And when she turned she saw the photos on the bureau, first time in how many years? Her young self as soft and pretty as a stranger. In another frame her husband with a basket of apples. And in the last a skinny boy at the beach. Her son. Such a smile.

Nearly broke her heart—three photos, three separate frames, each under its own glass—and from nowhere her father came back to her, man pretending to search for her and her sister, two little girls hiding under the dining room table, giggles rising like champagne bubbles in her throat, lace hanging over the side, giving everything a soft focus as he growled and stomped around the chairs. She remembered her father dying, those drowning eyes of her mother.

Hours, days she lay in the bedroom like this—years she stared at the cream ceiling, shadows of bugs in the frosted light fixture—and in that strange Darwinism of memory she thought of her son chopping at the fruit trees, the boy in tears over the greenhouses, how he said he thought they could float away. She could lie here and walk through the greenhouses and gardens in her mind, a hush of plants and leaves as she went, the old woman bending to listen for echoes all her life, waiting always for the safety of sadness to return, the tired comforts of loss and grief.

She closed her eyes—and why couldn't she lie a little longer here?—try to imagine it all happy for a change, her presentiments lifting like air in the curtains, her son riding home on a train, her husband in the seed shed as always. She could see the old man with his pollination charts, see him sorting seeds, bundles of drying plants hanging like sleeping bats above him, the hybridizer touching pollen from anthers to stamen, the man talking flowers to her in this dream, describing the rose he was trying to make, the feeling he was trying to bring to life for her, as if all her knots of worry might be untied with a scent or a softness. And in the dream she saw herself sleeping, her husband lying beside her, the two of them under the begonias, the last touches of daylight on the roof over them, glass all streaked and filmy, and that submarine tick and creak of the greenhouse as it cools with the deepening evening.

It surprised her, that knock of heels on the porch downstairs, the screen door opening, and she sat up as the hybridizer helloed into the living room for her. She got off the bed and stood at the window and listened to him in the kitchen, the water running in the sink, the woman like some attending angel over him. The man started up the stairs and she watched the clouded glass of the greenhouse below, part of her waiting for him to appear in the yard, part of her listening as he approached down the hall. She could feel him stop in the doorway, the volume he displaced in the room, and she swayed slightly and stared at the greenhouse, not wanting to miss his appearing on the lawn, the man already standing behind her.

What on earth are you doing? he asked.

She heard herself say hello to him—this faraway voice—

and it surprised her, the way she sounded. But what didn't surprise her these days? She was an old woman, prone to melancholy, and now she was suddenly full of strength, saying she was perfectly fine, in case he was wondering. She looked up at the ceiling and felt capable of anything, as if anything could fly out of her. All she had to do was open her mouth and turn to him.

Seriously, he said, you been sniffing those fertilizers again?

I have such wonderful news, she said, and smiled as she looked at him. You're going to be so happy, she said, so happy I'm not even going to tell you.

And she floated across the room and nudged the man from the door, bumped him along the hall and down the stairs and out of the house to the potting shed. Go on, she told him. Go make a nice vegetable or something.

He laughed as she flapped her hands to scare him off, laughed to see her standing in the yard, the old woman waiting for him to disappear into the greenhouse before she returned to her shop. And in the shop, a lone moth pattered at the light bulb, each bump and brush only making things worse. If she was crying now, at least she was crying for something happy this time, crying and laughing for this surprise she'd carry out to the hybridizer soon.

Crows in the orchard again, she could hear them, and they seemed reason enough to let herself go, woman tidying the shelves as she wept, the shop with its sad clutter and quiet. And then that *jing-jang* of bells, the door opening, and the auctioneer with his arms full of little dog. What's wrong? he asked when he saw her. Why are you crying?

It's nothing, she told him—but even the dog went quiet—
the whole shop going dry and airless as she tried to smile this
omen aside, the old woman saying that nothing was wrong.
She fluttered over some gladioli and laughed at herself and
wiped her face and held out her hands to show her fingers
shaking and nervous.

Everything's absolutely fine for once, she said. And this
must frighten me more than anything. Idea of being happy. I
mean, my son's coming home. Train gets in tonight. And look
at me now. Complete wreck.

She almost began to cry again, and the auctioneer set the
dog on the floor and put his arms around her, the man all wires
and pulleys as he hugged her, his voice tipping up with how
perfect, how wonderful, how lovely this was. May I tell my
mother? he asked.

Of course you may.

She'll be so thrilled, he said—and he pulled open the
door—the hybridizer standing in the bright of the driveway
by the car, the auctioneer's mother in the passenger's window,
the dog already across the grass to them. On the front steps
the auctioneer offered his arm, and the hybridizer's wife felt
herself carried by him, an effervescence of air and leaves and
trees, her body going soft and light as a girl as she leaned up
to the auctioneer. Don't tell him about my son, she whispered.
Still a surprise.

The man squeezed her hand to say yes—and then they were
at the car—the auctioneer saying what great news as he pulled
away, he and his mother waving goodbye, the hybridizer and
his wife standing in the drive, the two of them watching un-

til the car disappeared down the hill. The town seemed a toy model of a town below, rain clouds piling in the distance, and she could feel the hybridizer's hand go to the small of her back.

What was *that* all about? he asked.

Oh, you, she said—and she touched his chin—her fingertips to the rasp of his beard like a match being struck. Let's think of me as the little irritant that makes the pearl, she said, shall we?

Will do, he told her—and they started back toward the house—and again the crows in the orchard.

The birds were barking behind the gardens, calls so nagging and loud that she and the hybridizer circled around the porch to the sound. Past the gardens, past the greenhouses, and the crows weren't even birds out in the trees. More like splashes of ink against the light. One swinging up and around as if on a string. Sunlight like lace over the trees.

Caw, caw, caw.

Was hard to tell what the crows hated so much. No more than a handful of leaves. Some kind of squirrel's nest in the branches. The hybridizer and his wife edging forward until they stood directly under the tree. Crows loud, then quiet, then loud again. A beehive, a clot of gypsy moths, the hybridizer and his wife trying to see, and then this pale mask swiveled around to them, face as flat as a disk.

An owl!

She said it again—an owl—and the hair on her arms went electric. Those eyes just staring down. Tree so still it trembled. Bird smaller than she'd have thought. And then the crows started up again. Perhaps they never stopped, loud and

66

crass, harsh the way they hounded the poor thing. And all the while this face—such eyes—entire lifetime passing before its head tilted up again. Everything had moved closer in the dusk, and the owl loosened itself from the tree, dropped forward and started away toward the woods.

Even the crows fell quiet, owl strong and straight to that deep blue of trees in the distance, long strokes of its wings as it went. And the crows—so black they shone—one by one they started to peel away after the owl, feathers hissing as they rowed into the distance. And she felt herself in a dream as they followed—a dream she would have liked to dream—this strange dream where once upon a time an old woman emerged from a long dark wood.

GRISWALD

All you know is how sunny it was — so bright you could hardly see — and how this old man kept trying to tip you back into the stream, water breathless and cool, old Mr. Griswald standing behind you, his pants rolled up to his knees, his voice strange and far above, man saying not to worry, saying he has you, he has you.

This is going to be a terrible story. Can feel it coming already — that sinking sensation whenever he returns like this — the two of you entertaining the idea of space under the shade of his porch, your mother at work in the afternoons, your father who knows where. The Elks, the Lions, it hardly matters anymore. All that matters is this boy — you — eight or nine years old, old enough to take care of yourself apparently, aren't you? Only an hour before your mother gets home from work. Can always call the department store if you need to. Can always run to the neighbors if something bad happens.

And what's so wrong with wandering over to the old man's yard, anyway? He'll appear with bottles of soda. Old man quick to invite you onto the porch, quick to show what he's found while rummaging in the basement last night: an accordion, a wind-up-clock mechanism, an old telephone with magnets and coils of copper.

Any boy would have kept going to this porch. One day you're leaping from the back steps of his house, lost in musty parachutes, cloth around you like clouds. He flew in the war, old man telling how he was wounded, showing how bits of metal are still embedded in the scars, slivers of gray he picks from the skin of his elbow. He keeps the shards in a baby-food jar that he shakes like a rattle at you.

So it's parachutes one afternoon, swing sets in the park the next, the old man coaching you to pump your legs and swing higher, that moment of weightlessness at the top of each arc, the old man hollering if you can feel it there, and then right there? And you traipse into town with the man, the library ladies knowing all about him, two of you scuttling around to the racks of newspapers and magazines. His reading glasses are thick and filmy, frames bent out of shape, and his hands shake as he turns the pages, books about astronauts and satellites and planets and dark empty space, maps of the moon, charts of the stars. He reads an explanation of gravity to you and calculates your weight on each of the planets. On the moon you'd weigh 11 pounds. On Jupiter you'd weigh more than 160. In space you'd float weightless, no gravity at all. He says that would be something — weightlessness — and he musses your hair to start you home. We should go, he says, before anyone gets too worried about you.

Somewhere along the line you wonder aloud to him if it's actually possible — if you could travel in space one day — and the old man's teeth are so yellow they look green when he smiles, his hand on your shoulder as you walk together, the man saying, What a sweet boy you are.

Anything's possible, he says, this man so kind to you, his hand at the collar of your shirt.

Maybe you remind him of someone. Maybe it's that receding chin of yours. Whatever the reason, you arrive in his yard like a lost dog, and he calls you kiddo and hands you a glass of iced tea and asks what he can show you today. He proposes to get you ready, the old man promising to prepare you for your future, your destiny, your ultimate escape.

And now it's a story on the news, a sprinkler in a yard in the sunlight, a yellow school bus with its lights flashing, something always brings you back to the old man like this. All you really remember is how sunny it was, old man explaining how astronauts trained in water, how you could approach weightlessness this way, lying back in the stream, sun straight above and so bright and warm, stones slippery with algae, and him standing in the water behind you, saying not to worry, he has you, holding you by the wrists, saying he has you, he has you.

And years from this place, you're still not sure what he's trying to do with you exactly. Even now you worry what you're feeling as the water strokes your back and legs. Even now you tell yourself it's nothing at all. Just an old man trying to be nice to a boy. A lonely man, a lonely boy, the sun so bright you can hardly see, that cold, mentholated feel of the air after you get out of the stream and start home, this little kid crossing the street in his underwear, little kid carrying his clothes in his arms, sensing something is wrong, something about that hangdog look of the man, this scrawny little boy hurrying across the lawn on tiptoe.

And this boy—you—he never told anyone what happened, because maybe nothing happened, maybe it was nothing at all, and maybe it's still nothing at all. All these years later and maybe it's just a strange accident the way he returns to you like this, your father calling him a scrubby old queer, your father calling to him from the front walk, calling loud enough for the whole neighborhood to hear, your father standing there as if daring the old man to step out of his house, taunting the old man to appear to us, wishing he'd step out of that goddamn house.

And the rest of your life, it seems, you pretend not to notice the old man on his porch, feign distraction as you pass his house, old Griswald waving for you to come over, you almost not even noticing him, as if a stranger lives in that house, as if you don't know the chess set on his coffee table, the magazines in piles by his chair, the smell of stale tobacco in his couch, as if you don't watch that house of his in the moonlight, those yellow windows awake all hours of the night, those shades drawn, those rooms unable to fall asleep either, no one having to know about this little boy watching, no one having to see this little kid lying in bed like this, no one else having to know these nights all stuffy and sleepless, these nights not existing at all, these days not happening, nothing ever happening—and nothing still happening—nothing happening forever, right?

THIN END OF THE WEDGE

We were always something. All sorts of trouble, according to Joy-Dee, little mischief-makers, little pain-in-the-ass dickheads. We'd go open-handed to her, girl bribing us with candy, coins, television, bribing us with glimpses of her cotton-white underwear, bribing us with smiles so sly and pretty to us, girl promising to leave us alone if we left her alone, shooing us away as she talked on the phone—us being Kenny, Kiki, and me, ages eleven, nine, and eight—two brothers and me, their mascot, the three of us always hovering around, always hoping to get some reaction out of her, always wanting to see her all shrill and harried and chasing us across the yard, those short shorts and long legs, a high school senior with soft brown hair and smooth tanned skin, Joy-Dee trying to reason with us, trying to bargain with us, trying to explain the rules of the summer to us, her job to make sure that we didn't kill or maim one another on her watch.

And what else do you need to know? Want to know how later that next winter their house would burn down? Should I tell how they moved a few exits north, just across the state line, just far enough to never quite see the Hamiltons again? And how about the odd occasion that brings me home again now—a funeral or holiday—and that strange pull of this kid I used to be? Can I tell how I can't help but drive down the old street and expect to see that big rambling house from my memory, that dull white paint of the clapboards rubbing onto our hands, that third-floor attic room we used to play in? In its place is the same disappointment of raised ranch that has stood there for the past thirty years—dull brown face of the house saying, Don't look at me, kid—sorry little carport shrugging me aside. The garage next door, the fence around the yard, the cars parked on the street, all of it saying, You've got the wrong place, saying, You're not remembering correctly, saying, You must be lost.

And it must be true, as the street itself tries to tell me, because the apple tree is gone as well, and next door squats another house where the aboveground pool used to be, and even the trees are not like I remember them. They strike me as small and misshapen now, stunted and diseased, most of them scooped and carved to make way for telephone and electric wires. Yet when I picture my childhood it takes place under big bouquets of elms and oaks and maples, shade spreading like picnic blankets over the grass and houses. The rest of the street might be familiar to me—those tired sags of the porches, the clotheslines, the garages, the furniture on the lawn—but it's the trees that make me wonder if I haven't been making

76

up everything in my mind, making it all so much better than it actually was.

I can accept that the people, the houses, the sidewalks have all changed or disappeared in the years since my father died, but for some reason I can't fathom the trees diminished as much as the rest of us. It makes me question much more than just trees, of course, because if I'm not remembering something as basic as those trees correctly, where does that leave my father? I mean, when did he actually leave my mother and me? How come I don't know something as basic as that? And why did my mother keep his pints of whiskey tucked under the kitchen sink? Did she open the caps at night—one breath of whiskey or aftershave bringing my father back to her—or am I only imagining this kind of longing? And where does this leave my mother? Her dripping faucet, her flooded basement, my mother blaming my father for everything wrong in her life, the woman nothing if not disappointment, her days solid-through with loss. And then what about me? From the trees to the Hamilton brothers to my father in that coffin, the man lying as if in a bath of flowers, have I been dreaming this up all along?

Strange, sad, scary how it won't lie still for me. Almost funny how I keep circling back to this—variations on a theme—my ur-story, my rhyming action, my template for everything that follows. That everything being my father gone, my mother wounded, and myself this boy trying to lay it all to rest somehow.

But maybe there's nothing to lay to rest—that absence so central to me that I may never be able to look at it directly—

and I'm hiding again in some fiction of trees that must spread healthy and huge over this boy's childhood. Easier to imagine these things present than to imagine them gone. The Hamilton brothers eating breakfast in the kitchen, the house standing so sturdy and bright, Mr. Hamilton leaving for work with his lunchbox, Mrs. Hamilton working in the department store with my mother, Joy-Dee sitting us for the summer.

As I recall, we were interested in the idea of turning the pool into a vortex. We scraped the powder out of firecrackers and flares to make a bomb out of a mailbox. We were these great little kids carrying out their one glorious summer together, three boys left to their own devices. And all I know is that for me — that boy of eight — his father's death would be more inconvenient than anything else.

One minute a boy might go all annoyed at being dragged away from his summer for the funeral, and the next he'd be grateful that the man was gone for good, no absence to explain away anymore, no mealy-mouthed excuses for the man, no trying to remember what story he said to whom. The boy no longer had to lie because now he had the truth to tell. His father was dead. Big deal.

Besides, if someone's father had to die, it might as well have been a father that no one would miss. Kenny and Kiki's father, Mr. Hamilton, he coached baseball, ran a scout troop, fixed bicycles in the yard, took his sons camping, washed and waxed his car on weekends. He even stopped as he left for work to ask if everything was all right with me. I was sitting on the side steps that morning, and he put his hand on my shoulder and said he was sorry about my father — he meant he was sorry about my father's death—and he said not to worry, that everything would be all right. I had to go to my father's wake that afternoon, and Mr. Hamilton turned to the house and hollered for his boys to get outside and play with Jeffrey before he had to leave.

A crab-apple tree reached over the pool—the Hamiltons had an aboveground pool, had a double lot for baseball, had a kind of shed with broken bikes, old appliances, tires, a heaven of scrap wood and old wheels and electric motors—and we started every morning by fishing apples out of the pool, skimming the scum bubbles that collected against the liner, the insects that swirled around in the foam. Anything particularly disgusting—a salamander, a drowned mole—we'd leave in the kitchen or next to the telephone. We loved to hear Joy-Dee go shrill, her voice a siren.

That day was like any other. We cleaned the pool, checked the chlorine, banged the bugs and leaves from the filter, all the usual chores. We must have thrown apples down the street, tossed them like golf balls onto the roof, that smell of apples so thick sometimes we could hardly breathe. Must have ended up playing baseball, the game always bringing out the brawls in us. It'd be me versus Kenny, Yankees versus Red Sox, archrivals with Kiki as the designated pitcher, the rattled southpaw, always more on my side than his brother's. Earlier, trying to be funny, Kenny had thrown my glove into the pool, and as payback Kiki unloaded a fastball that caught his brother on the side of his face. Took a while, Kenny on the ground, me and Kiki nervous and hectic, the two of us bouncing over the mound, calling him a drama queen, telling him to get up and fight. And when Kenny pushed himself off the grass, finally, he calmly said he was going to kill us, his face and shirt bright with blood.

And he meant it, aluminum bat in his hands, Kenny chasing his brother into the corner of the yard, stalking him to the back fence, and taking a swing—a hard, mean, full swing at his brother—Kiki with his hand up by reflex, the sound like a chicken wing snapping. He was cradling his arm, trying not to cry, his eyes wild and afraid. I don't know what came over me, but I rushed Kenny and tackled him from behind, started punching ears and twisting fistfuls of hair. And it was me making all the noise—I was the one crying and yelling and unable to stop—Joy-Dee across the yard, pinching my neck and lifting me away.

She moved between us. What the hell? she yelled. What the frick's with you?

I wiped my mouth and stared at her, the cords in her neck all tight, and she would have hit me if I hadn't stepped away. She said she'd slap that grin off my face if she saw it there for another goddamn second. I couldn't help it—I laughed—and she seemed shaken and not sure where to even start with me, Joy-Dee hesitant in a way that was new with us, as if we were dogs she didn't know or trust anymore, dogs that didn't back down or look away or care, dogs with our ears down and the hair on our necks up. And we must have understood this, because Kiki stood there, cradling his arm, and told his brother to drop dead and started running toward the street. I watched them watch him go—and then I flipped them the bird and followed Kiki, Kenny disappearing into the house with Joy-Dee,

Kiki and me in the yard by the pool. My hands trembled as I put them into the water and wet my face, Kiki trying to move his arm, the boy both crying and not crying at the same time.

Hard to say how much time went by—even then it was a blur—Joy-Dee coming outside with that long sad diaper face of hers, telling me it was time to get cleaned and dressed and ready to go, my mother out of work early that day, her Chevelle pulling into the driveway before lunch, and the next thing I knew I was sitting in the back seat, all clean and changed, wearing a brand-new suit and shirt, my hand held out of the open window, riding the air like a plane. We ate at a burger place on the way out of town, my mother and I, and then we were on the highway, me leaning forward in case my mother wanted to say anything to me.

Part of me hoped she'd take me aside and explain it all, part of me grateful she didn't say a word, my mother digesting her thoughts and her feelings alone.

We rode for miles of silence.

Companionable silence.

In a previous life our Chevelle had been a driver's education car, my mother never bothering to remove the extra brake on the passenger side. Not only was that a luxury we didn't need to spend the money on—or so she'd tell me—but the brake pedal gave her a simple excuse to keep me in the back seat, allow her some privacy as she drove. Perhaps my mother never liked me very much, perhaps I reminded her of my father, reminded her of what had gone wrong in her life. I don't even know what went wrong, but many times I felt that she'd have been better off without me, that I was a bad luck charm for her, a bad omen for them.

When I asked to be next to her, and promised not to touch the brake, she'd insist there wasn't any room, that the Holy Ghost liked to ride shotgun next to her, that she needed the space to spread out her things. Became a routine with us, my mother trying to joke me aside until she thought I forgot, her voice looping up high as she told me to keep myself occupied back there, to just let her drive for a while in peace, to let her concentrate please.

Pretty big front seat, Mom. Couldn't the three of us fit? You know, me, you, *and* the Holy Ghost. I'll be good. I promise.

No, no, she'd say, that's all right.

Lotta room up there, I'd say. Holy Ghost must be pret-ty massive.

Just be a good boy, she'd say. Just stay back there, please.

Well, actually, Mom, if he's so big maybe he'd be more comfortable in the rear. Whole back seat for him here, you know.

That's enough already, she'd say—and when she lifted her arm to the back of the seat and turned to look at me, I could see a dark ring of sweat in the armpit of her dress—and it put my heart in my throat for some reason, as if that triangle under her arm was an injury I could see and feel as my own.

We weren't driving far—little more than an hour to the farm in Franklin—the place where my father lived after he left. It's interesting to me now, all these years later, to think how close he was to us on a map, yet how little we saw of him. I don't remember, just for the record, ever really missing him, his absence not affecting me at all.

And no sooner does a sentence like that leave my lips than I feel that it's just another lie I tell myself, which I'm sure it is, a lie like the lie about the trees I must still have to believe. I never felt I needed my father, yet here I am again, casting back like this out of some deep sense of loss or deprivation, as if still trying to find a way into my father's heart, or still trying to make a place for him in mine.

I mean, why did we visit him only two times that I remember? Both occasions ending with me asleep on the couch in my clothes. A woodstove to my back. Their voices, my mother's and father's, all watery and distant in the next room. That swerve of her laugh. That can-do purr of his voice. That jib and jab of their voices lulling me to sleep.

And when I listen like this, I feel that even then they must have loved each other in their own way, just as I know somehow my father must have cared for me, the man slapping me upside the head, or showing me how to double-knot my shoes, or taking me fishing to the pond on the farm. I must have been six or seven years old — and perhaps I'm only dreaming this as well — the two of us standing in the dusk, watching as he attracted the bats with the whir of a fishing pole. He'd whip the pole, make the sound, and down swooped the bats.

It's something, he'd say, the way they come down, isn't it?

And the bats would dive toward us, thin and unsteady, the boy just watching, mouth open, the dusk making everything granular. And the man would toss stones into the air to show how the bats followed almost to the water, poor things pulling up at the last moment, the man play-swatting his son on the back of the legs with the pole. The boy's eyes might betray him, might blur with tears, but his mouth he could keep pressed tight as a line.

His father could laugh — big throaty laugh of a man — and the boy could look away to the house, the windows, his mother behind those curtains somewhere. And where was she now? What was she doing all by herself in his house? Why wasn't she with us? How was the boy here alone with his father?

C'mon, answer your old man, he'd say.

What d'you want me to say, Dad?

Along the highway, the trees flared past and the stone walls snaked into and then out of the woods. Had a history of carsickness and rode with the window half open, my hand an airplane again, banking and rising with the road. Got those telltale strands of saliva, taste of burger and fries in my mouth, all the feelings I couldn't quite swallow away, and my mother'd start asking if I was okay back there, telling me to keep my eyes on the road in front. I'm just fine, I'd tell her, but the Holy Ghost could use some more air. Not really looking so hot. Paper bag to his mouth. Should've let me sit up in front with you, Mom.

She'd look at me in the rearview mirror. Almost there, she'd say.

The funeral home was in Baltic, and the parking lot had fake puddles, mirages from the heat, the house an old Victorian with scalloped siding and a turret, traffic cones out front, the lawn the green of frozen peas. It was sunny and warm and we were standing beside the car, my mother and me, glare off the windshield, the woman with her hand on my shoulder, an awkward, unnatural moment, her leaning her weight against me, as if she needed something to hold her up, as if I was suddenly the sturdiest thing in her life.

And what did I do?

I pulled away from her.

I stepped aside, told her go by herself, that I'd be fine out here alone.

She looked at me, stared as if to ask where I'd learned to talk like this, only to realize that she knew where I'd learned, my mother bending to kiss the top of my head, as if to forgive me, as if to forgive herself. Her whole body seemed to relax, her shoulders, her face, her hands, everything better if I stayed out by the car like this, my mother turning on her heel and starting across the lot toward the awning and front door. She went inside. There were birds and trees and sky to watch, and I traced the hood, the fender, the roof of our car. Not too long, and this man stepped out of the funeral home. He lit a cigarette, smoke trailing behind as he made his way across the lot. He looked like a younger, slightly heavier version of my father — same nose, same squint, same part of hair to one side — his smile a watered-down version of my father's and my own.

He was my uncle Daniel, and was holding his hand out to me, his hand like a catcher's mitt in mine.

And what, I wonder, could he have said to me, besides how nice the weather was, how warm the sun, how soon would school be starting again? And those Red Sox, he said, what did I think of them this year? And what could I—an eight-year-old kid—what should I have asked of him, truly? My father's brother, what would I want to know or not know from him? If the same meeting happened today—if my thirty-nine-year-old self could stand in for that boy—if I could return to him now, I'm not so sure I'd hold up better than I did back then. The older me would probably fill that silence with small talk about who knows what? The wires in Joy-Dee's neck when she got mad, my baseball glove like a turtle at the bottom of the pool, God knows what kind of nonsense I'd pull.

But the boy was perfect. He stood there silent and calm, his uncle flicking that cigarette away, asking if he'd ever been to a ball game. I'll drive up, said the man, see if we can't get your mother to come with us. You a Red Sox fan?

The boy shrugged.

Luis Tiant? Carlton Fisk? Butch Hobson?

The boy said he was more a Yankees fan, and the man smiled and tut-tutted him. A car pulled into the lot—a Bonneville, big and blue—and the boy's uncle said to hang tight, he'd be right back. The man crossed to the other car, and the boy looked away to the sky, which was empty and bright and blue. He tapped the antenna of the car and tried to think of what to think of next. His father, fishing, bats, and the word *nocturnal,* meaning that they slept during the day. And *mammal,* meaning that they were warm-blooded. *Echolocation,* meaning they saw by sending clicks from their mouth or nose and listening to the sound bouncing back from trees or insects or stones thrown into the air. All seemed incredible, the things of the world, and sometimes it was all a boy could do to believe that a fish breathed water, or that a butterfly flew all the way from Mexico, or that water froze into ice, or any of the seemingly endless miracles of the universe. Everything, if you looked closely enough, was a mystery. The most normal things, the most obvious things in the world, the things we took most for granted, often these were the most impossible, the most mysterious.

Uncle Daniel produced a quarter from behind my ear when he returned. You must have dropped this, he said, and tickled more coins from the nape of my neck. I squirmed, flinched away from him, held out my hands when he jingled a fistful of change to me.

Look at that, he said, got the same grin as your father, don't you?

He shook his head and let his smile melt away—a car passed on the street—and my uncle handed me the change and said I should come inside and be with the family for a little while. I took the money, put it in my pocket, and followed him toward the house, into the funeral home. Was like stepping into winter, that foyer, the air conditioning so cold, the hushed way everyone seemed to move, it all seemed snowbound inside.

And from the doorway, I had everything I needed: my mother in her black dress by the windows, soft clutter of flowers, the spotlights on, people talking, music low, and my father lying in the midst of it all, as if asleep in the bath.

Like my uncle, I dipped my fingers into the pedestal of water, made the sign of a cross, and kissed my fingertips. Strange, but it seemed my eyes touched things, everyone turning when I looked at them. My mother must have felt my glance on her shoulder, and she crossed the room to me, whispered something in my ear, though all I heard was the feathers of her breath. She tried to turn me from the room, but I was already moving toward him, my father drawing me forward, against my will, until I was standing where everyone must have stood, this little kid pretending to pray. Felt my father trying to steal things from me, things that I needed, like my mouth, which couldn't open, like my legs, which couldn't move, like my lungs, my ability to breathe all of a sudden gone.

It was awful, and I could see that he had rouge on his cheeks, that his lips were red like lipstick, that his face seemed made of candle wax, cheeks molded smooth by thumbs. Not supposed to touch the face of a dead person, even if it was your own father, even if you were trying to turn him into a thing, your hand reaching forward slowly, just to make sure, his hair hard and sticky with spray.

My mother drove us home that afternoon, sun in dots and dashes through the trees, radio tuned to pianos. We rode quiet together, not saying anything for almost the whole highway. I pretended to be so tired in the back seat, didn't want her to explain or ask anything. I didn't want reasons or excuses, didn't want her, didn't want him, didn't even want myself. A turn, a traffic light, and eventually we were on our street and in our driveway, her face sad and heavy as she stood in the yard, and I wanted for some reason to add to that pain of hers, as if she could carry more guilt and regret and anger on her face, as if she should be punished even more for this.

Are you hungry? she asked. What would you like for dinner?

Nothing, I said.

You coming in?

No, I told her, not yet.

She let me stay outside as long as I wanted that night. The woods that bordered the yard were the Green Monster, Yankees playing away tonight, the lawn being Fenway, dusk flooding our house, our car in the drive, our neighborhood. Never failed to be the ninth inning, Yanks versus Sox, all tied up yet again. Stepping up to the plate, batting third, the catcher, number 15, Thur-man Mun-son. The spark, the soul, the heart of New York. One out, Bucky Dent on second, Mickey Rivers on first, and I was Munson. All scrappy and stocky. I picked stones from the gravel of our driveway and hit them into the trees with a baseball bat—that was what only children did, they invented games and ghost runners and went extra innings alone in the dark—and Munson drilled a hanging curve deep into the leaves for a double, Yaz playing it off the wall, the crowd in a fanfare of wind. The trees knew the truth when they saw it, the way they cheered and chanted in the air. Dent home for the go-ahead, Rivers holding up on third, Munson dusting his pants on second, whatever he lacked in legs or size he made up for in heart and that trucker's mustache and sideburns of his. After his plane went down—the man practicing takeoffs and landings in his jet—the team wore armbands of

Yankee blue to honor him because they'd loved him, needed him, and wished he was still there, felt the hole that he left in the lineup.

Our house sat a little up the hill from the driveway and my mother stood in the kitchen doorway, leaning against the screen. Getting dark, I heard her say. She was right, I told her. It's what happens at night, Mom. Gets dark.

And I don't like this kid very much right here either—but I do love him—and I do wish him well, just as I wish for my father, and wish for my mother, the woman saying, Dinner's ready, saying, Why don't you come in now, hon?

Me pretending not to hear a single word.

Her saying, At least put a jacket on.

I'm okay, Mom.

And low over the one light in the yard, I'm seeing things —small gray bats—they skitter against the sky, tissuey and tense. Standing in the grass, lawn wet and cold, trees feathering dark, I'm standing right here, yet I feel like I'm no longer here at all, this boy dissolving into the darkness, like he's slowly turning into the darkness itself, a handful of air in the air.

Look! he says.

I see!

Bats!

Hated to confuse the bats like this, but it's all so fantastic, me pulling the bats from the sky, them crying after the stones that they take for food, everything so tense and tenuous. Would have loved to show Kiki and Kenny how over and over I do this, would have loved to teach them to throw the stones just ahead of the bats, the bats with that clicking sound of theirs, me constantly disappointing the poor things, the creatures pulling up at the last second and skittering away. And there I am, small stones in my hands, this kid swaying slightly as he stands alone, feeling like his father must have felt, saying, Nice, aren't they?

And when no one says anything, he hits me—not hard— my father knocking me on the back of the head. Answer your old man, he says.

I *see* them already, I say. I mean, what d'you want me to say?

Say they're nice or something, that's all.

They're nice already.

There you go, he says—and he smiles and looks up to the sky, the trees—and then he looks to me again. Now, he says, why was *that* so hard?

Killed a deer last night. Kate and me and this creature almost completely over us. Flash of animal, tug of wheel, sound
we felt more than heard, poor thing lying on the side of the
road as we pulled around.

Should have just kept driving, gone home, felt bad. Don't
know what possessed us to get out of the car. November and
nothing but trees around. No cars, no houses, deer small and
slender, tongue powdered with sand. Kate stood in the col-
umn of headlight, her shadow a stick in water, her hand reaching as if to untangle its legs, shoo the thing away. Such a well-
traveled stretch of road, and still no one drove past as we
struggled the animal onto an old blanket. Weren't thinking it
through, obviously, but there must have been something very
desperate in us, something full of yearning, two of us lifting
the deer into the trunk, object more awkward than heavy.

Called the police, the game warden, would call Billy in
the morning, give him something to laugh about down at the

Elks. Crazy neighbors bringing their roadkill home, stringing it up in a tree for the night, asking what they should do next.

Sure, he'd say, be right over.

Billy Hawkins owns the farm down the road from us. Ninety acres of pastures and hayfields, broken-down trucks and barns. Used to keep dairy cows, like his father, but gets paid more *not* to milk these days. No need to elaborate, towns around here changing. Condos and golf courses, pastel mansions in the middle of cornfields, old mills becoming antique shops and restaurants. Billy scoffs at it all—hard not to take it personally—hobby farmer that he's become, few Herefords for tax purposes, truck of his all nice and clean.

We expect him to arrive with the reasons we shouldn't be doing this, as if we need permission to give up on the deer. Maybe the meat is tainted, ruined by blood, spoiled through some neglect we don't know about. Hope he will just smile and shake his head and suggest we bury the damned thing. Kate will laugh with relief. I'll joke about our own stupidity and go fetch a shovel. That's what we hope, at least.

Hardly seems worth the effort by morning, deer so slight, awful how she holds that stretch as we cut her down. Billy drives up and grabs a leg, saying, Gimme paw. He laughs, motions us across the yard, tells us to dump her by the shed, Kate taking the wheelbarrow as I tip the animal to the grass.

Careful, whispers Billy, don't want to wake her up or anything now, do you?

And again that laugh—that big, infectious, china-rattling laugh—Billy pulling a pair of yellow kitchen gloves from his jacket. He opens a knife, blade the length of a finger, and lowers himself next to the deer, taps the drum of the animal's stomach.

So, he says to us, eaten much venison in your day?

We say no, of course, and squint against the light.

At least *not yet* we haven't, says Kate.

Billy touches the ground for balance and twists the animal by the neck until the body follows, man asking me to kneel down and hold her steady, deer on its back, legs spread, hair thin and delicate. Billy tells how it's best to open these things right away, how skin tends to keep heat, how organs bleed out sometimes. He lifts the tail and explains how you start by cutting around the anus. Want to free the whole circle of it, he says — and that liquid crackle of knife as he works — Billy saying, You can't nick the colon, can't nick the bladder, want to pull the whole intestinal tract in one fell swoop from the body.

He stops to tighten his gloves and cleans the blade on the plush of the deer. Shows how to hold the knife for this, finger on top of the blade, blade bright and sharp. Moves to the chest of the animal, his pants wet at the knees, and Billy plucks the thin underside of hair, says there's a tender spot along the brisket, pinches the skin between his fingers, and starts to tick the point of the knife away from himself. The flesh opens like a zipper, entire suit of the deer in one long draw of blade, Billy like a steam engine working.

Maybe it's the way he breathes through his nose, sound of steel wool in his nostrils, but he reminds me of those uncles who were never really uncles, Uncle Eddie or Uncle Walter, the sort of men my brother and I would try to borrow as fathers. We'd try to hand the right tools as they fixed a door or snaked a drain, men rationing their affection, withholding their praise, asking if we were behaving for our mother, teasing if we had girlfriends yet, slipping us a few dollars for our help. Some spending money, they'd say. Can't go around begging your whole life, can you?

Animal would have stayed on its back by now, but I hold her anyway, that musky smell of hooves, man slicing through the deer's milk sacks, milk running to the grass. Billy pushes the blade between the animal's legs until he connects, at last, to that first round cut at the tail. Rest goes quickly enough. Lungs, liver, intestines, everything on the grass, heart like a knot of wet rags. Kate's stepped back from this, cold sweet taste of metal in the air, smudge of blood on Billy's sleeve, man scraping the cage of ribs as if cleaning the inside of a pumpkin.

He dangles the esophagus and asks if I want to feel. I shake my head no—and he turns to Kate—and she steps forward as if to take a garden hose, as if she's made some kind of deal, some kind of promise to see this through to the end. Billy peels the gloves off his hands and helps string the animal up in the tree, deer more like a deer again, feet tied together, legs stretched, Billy about to leave.

I'll call my buddy Andy, he says. Owns a little grocery, can butcher the thing for us, see if we can't finish her off this afternoon.

Kate begs off whatever's left of this—the flushing out of the body, the intestines and lungs to clean from the grass, the slaughtering of the animal—and she hands me the phone

when Billy calls. You know, he says, lucky if we get twenty
pounds of meat off her. Wouldn't be bad to just stay home, be
good boys for a change, make nice to our wives maybe?

Up to you, I tell him. I mean, you're the one doing us the
favor, but weren't you going to get hold of your friend?

I did, he says—and there's this catch in his voice—and I
can see him take a breath over the phone. All right, he says,
toss her in the trunk and swing by the house.

Now this is where I am supposed to go find Kate upstairs,
that soft and tender moment between us, where I give the
comfort she wants and needs. That wicker creak of quiet,
house holding its breath, and I know exactly what to do, but
for some reason I'm calling up the stairs that I gotta run—and
I'm out the door—and I'm in the yard again, sun so bright it's
painful, afternoon so clear and cool I could drink it.

And don't think it doesn't cross my mind to just keep driving past Billy's house. Don't think, as I load the deer into the
car, that I don't want to skip this entire thing, skip the small
talk with Billy's wife, the cup of coffee, the can of beer. Don't
think I want any of this, Billy directing me from the Lions to
the Elks to the Knights of Columbus until we find his friend,
the three of us switching to Andy's truck, deer in the back
with plywood and buckets of road salt and sand. Few miles
to the little grocery where Andy starts in on the deer, whine
of circular saw cutting the animal's feet off, taste of burned
bone in the room, another beer from the freezer, broken bi-
cycle of carcass to carry to the garbage. Don't think I need
the dark outside like this, either, the cold clean air of alley, the
smell of game on my hands, Billy and Andy laughing about

something inside, that endless dream of fitting in with men like these, standing easy with them, chores all but done, that look of thirst on our faces, blood on our aprons, just rinsing counters at this point, wiping down knives, and let's get out of here.

I carry the wrapped cuts of deer in a carton, meat going in back with the plywood, Andy and Billy waiting for me to join them again. Only I'm moving away from the truck, telling them to go on, saying I want to walk home. Middle of the parking lot and they look at me like I've just appeared from behind the dumpsters, hungry dog with some scent in the air. C'mon, says Billy, quick stop at the Elks, can pick up your car at least.

But I'm almost to the street by now, trying not to hurry around the first corner, hiding in the shrubs until the truck is gone. Oh, champagne air—oh, dark empty streets—oh, I'm running and laughing and crying and telling Kate this whole story. Can run forever, it feels, past all these sleeping houses, sky wild with stars, crazy person down the middle of the street with blood on his hands, up to his elbows in this mess.

CALVARY

Lifted the grocery bag off the hood of the car and got in behind the wheel and unlocked the passenger side for the boy and all the clocks started forward again. The two of them glided out of the parking lot, slow down the hill and avenue, looking for her on either side of the street. First set of lights and he sent the boy into a deli for some coffee and a pack of cigarettes. By the time the kid came out of the store, his father had already turned the car around to the far side of the street. He watched the boy cross the traffic, this gangly eleven-year-old kid around the front of the car, and they drove back up the hill toward the cemetery, eased in through the open gates, angels on either side of them, stone wall rough and tall and covered with graffiti.

One lazy turn after another and the man steered the old Plymouth through the endless wreckage of pillars and statues, crosses and columns, trees, crypts, the hills crowded with stones. At the crest of the hill the city lay beyond, buildings jumbled and shining, like another cemetery in the distance. The lanes went cinder and narrow and the man idled at a long cul-de-sac of great tall elms, the graves and cobblestones all heaved askew by the roots beneath, the shade like damp blankets over the grass, the man parking under the trees.

Shall we? he asked.

And when the boy didn't say anything, the man nudged his shoulder. C'mon, let's walk.

They got out of the car. Glimpses of distance through the stones. Sound of an airplane. And then quiet. The boy followed his father—so quiet in this place—that dry tinsel of grass under his feet. The boy felt whispers brushing close as they went. Sunlight through the trees. Air warm and heavy as bath water. Drifted behind the man, sky almost viscous, the boy watching himself from above, as if all of this had happened before, was happening again, just as he'd dreamed it. The headstones, the dwarf pines, the pots and plants and pictures and ribbons, the tiny graves of children like milk teeth in the grass, the brick chapel he was just on the verge of remembering as it appeared before them.

The man called back how he was thinking about some flowers and the boy looked to his father, man wavery in the light, voice far away and nasal and not quite connected to the person standing there. The boy stared at him, never seen this person before in his life, it seemed, a stranger in dress trousers and boots, shirt pressed, hair slick and shining in the sun, hands on hips, head tipping to one side slightly.

Strange fucking kid, said the man, aren't you?

The boy shrugged and continued to his father, kept walking past the man as if carried by some slow undertow, the two of them floating up the hill toward the chapel ahead of them, shush of the footsteps as they went, trees so vivid and green they sparkled, each leaf its own little leaf, the hair on the boy's arms crawling like insects.

She was close. Expected any moment to see her. Chapel sold flowers and candles and the boy's father picked one of the wreaths from the rack at the top of the steps. Slipped money into the metal strongbox, coins like ice in a glass, and those dress boots hard and crackling and loud on the stone steps.

Stood like this forever, two of them on the steps of that little chapel for the rest of their lives. Calvary Cemetery, a snapshot, and years from this place the boy—no longer a boy—he'd come back and find them there, man smoking a cigarette, boy kicking at the rail with the toe of his shoe, his father pressing the wreath onto the kid at last.

Here you go, he'd say, the man's voice out of sync with his mouth, the boy taking the flowers, the hoop of Styrofoam, smell of glue, the carnations like lips to the kid's cheek. His father let out a long breath of exasperation and snapped his fingers and started them into the chapel.

Inside was cool and dim and cellar damp, taste of candle wax, boy inching his way until his eyes adjusted to the dark, flickering candles in red cups ahead of them, stained-glass windows to each side, sunlight through rubies and pharmacy-bottle blues, his father's heels like a clock ticking down the smooth stone of the floor. Always the click of those heels on the floor, man down the aisle, man dipping his fingers in the font, crossing himself, kissing his fingertips as if to slip a key into his mouth.

And the boy pressed the flowers to his face and edged down the center aisle, the darkened rows of pews, high vaulted ceiling above him, scuff of pigeons inside, his father circling to the side aisle and altar. A few more steps and one of the pews creaked beside the boy, a chill shooting past him, someone in the shadows, the outline of someone in the dark.

Couldn't seem to take a breath, couldn't seem to move, the boy trying to turn away, trying to not see anything, his mother sitting there, darkness in the dark. He missed her so much—was awful—another piece falling into place wrong, boy's mother slowly turning to him, gentle smile of hers, kind of veil over her face, her features hard to see in the shadows. Her mouth—and again that dream of his—his mother's breath like hair against his face. Hey, pumpkin, she was saying, her voice small, how you been?

Tried to hold himself up, hand on the pew, the straight-backed pew, didn't dare let go, didn't dare move, murmurs like water running just beneath the surface of the wood. And the boy watched his mother, watched himself staring at her, footsteps approaching down the aisle, boy turning to the man, and the vision—if you could call it that—vanished.

His father wouldn't see her sitting there, of course, and he'd nudge the boy forward, pew empty, sunlight framed by the doors, man making some joke about the wreath, about the kid not eating the damned thing already, man laughing up toward the ceiling, sound multiplying loud in the space, boy with that acid burn of soap in his mouth.

Outside the sun was blinding, boy holding the rail down the steps, his father on the cinder path ahead of him. The man lit a cigarette and touched a speck of tobacco off his tongue, gathered himself, looked across at the matching stones of nuns, all of them lined perfect. Nice of them to put all the sisters together, he tried to joke, wouldn't you say?

Already the boy was away from all of this in his mind, riding with his father out of the cemetery again, driving all the stop-and-go streets of the world, the wide boulevards past car dealers and discount stores, past cream-brick tenements and gas stations, his father at the wheel, the city devolving into an almost endless edge of town. Ice cream in their future. A diner and some supper. A filling station with die-cast metal rocket ships to coax his father into buying for him. This lonesome, sad, spoiled-rotten kid of his. That wounded look as good as money.

His father started counting down the markers — section 33, row 33 — and the stone lay a short walk away. A small neighborhood of tombs, back-to-back like summer cottages, statues and crosses, glimpses of the city in the distance. Crest of the hill and the view went long. A flyover of expressway, oil containers, smokestacks and steeples and rooftops, the skyline transparent in the haze, and this kid rubbing beads of Styrofoam from the back of the wreath, the man's hand going to his shoulder, the boy slipping out from under him.

He followed his father, wishing all the while that he could

step out of himself, let the man go with the empty costume of a boy in his hand. The real boy—whoever that was—would huddle himself small and lost alongside the statues and stones, watch his father disappear, skin of a boy dragged across the ground behind the man.

LOVE IS A TEMPER

Leaving was simple. He and his father had only to walk to the train station, the two men embracing when the train arrived, Joseph tapping his pockets for his papers, boarding the train, and watching as the old man shrank into the blue of steam and distance, his father's arm raised to say goodbye, all of it like a fairy tale, like a story told for children.

Leaving was easy, the raw movement of it, and the dark Ukrainian fields opened out full and spread the sky wide with light. Immense hours of plowland and trees and the country hilly and wild. Once upon a time, they traced switchbacks over the Carpathians by night, changed trains in Bucharest, and pushed past more bare trees and graying farms and distance, the incessant skip of wheels and rails and movement, each detail deserving a story of its own — the lines of poplars, the loud metal bridge, the people working in fields stopping to watch the train pass, the children waving, and then the mountains like the moon, always with him when he looked up. Together it all drew sounds from his chest—animal growls and groans—Joseph telling how he pulled the window open and washed his face in the wind, the sounds rising out of his throat as if the land were using him to speak.

And all of this turned blue with distance and time, as blue as the voyage across the ocean, nothing but shades of blue for days on days, days and blue as heavy as the drone of the engines and the sea and the stories he'd carry like souvenirs. Like the story of the woman who brought the baby over to America. God, just the word—*America*—the idea alone held them all like a dream and a promise big enough to hold anyone who could say it. It was everyone's story: each version a leaving, a rumbling of trains, a ship under way, glimpses of weather, all the great longings that never seemed to rest, and the stories that never went still, like the woman with that baby of hers, the way he'd never know her name, yet her face?

Her face, he would say, her face carried the sea in it—cold, gray, unstable.

In one breath he could describe how the sea moved through moods, and in the next he could tell how, in the steerage below deck, the mother never set her child down, how she kept it nestled in the long folds of her skirt, rocked it, sang softly to it, smiled without showing her teeth, as if it pained her to smile. Joseph would say how he might have been falling in love with her as she slept beside him, her mouth open, her teeth black.

His voice soft, he could tell that the baby was dead, its

hands stiff and curled, the woman keeping it close as a doll. She bumped the child and hummed to it and pretended to hear the small noises of an infant, Joseph trying all the while not to watch. He'd leave them below and stand on deck in the clean, clear, cold air outside, a horizon of water and glare. He'd bring her a tin of food that evening, the baby in her lap as she ate, the rocking of the ship awful that night.

And when she motioned for the water, Joseph would sit on the floor at her feet and lean to hand the cup to her, touching the woman's arm and holding it, keeping his hand on her, pressing as if to break a spell and wake her.

A statue's stare, her face hard and blank and far beyond him—and the next time she moved she'd break—though Joseph would never explain how she broke, or what this meant, only that she was a statue, that she emptied linens from a trunk, and that she swaddled the baby in nice white blankets. She carried the bundle topside up onto the deck, and Joseph followed a few steps behind, not knowing what else to do, the woman finding the rail at the end of the ship, standing there in the clothlike light of the moon. In some ways, he'd already be wondering if there had ever been a child? Was this woman even real? She seemed almost transparent in the light as she let the bundle fall over the side of the ship.

And if he faltered, if he couldn't tell the story again, the girls would turn to their mother. She could continue to the end because it was true, and because it was their story now, and because she had heard or imagined this so many times that it became her own crossing, as if she'd been there with him from the start, as if she felt everything he felt as he stood with that woman at the rail.

She could tell the happier occasions too—a glimpse of dolphins, a brick of chocolate from Vienna—Ellen describing the way rain falls into the ocean, both resisted and replenishing at the same time, the surface of the sea all hammered and thin as a precious metal. She could tell how Joseph carried the diamond across the ocean with him, how he held it in his mouth instead of in his pocket, and how he once swallowed and waited for it to pass through him. The girls would squeal—they'd squirm at the thought—and Joseph would lift their mother's hand to the light, the stone perfect and blue, and Ellen hesitant to show the ring, afraid to tempt fate with such happiness.

The ring would stand for so many things to her, their story being everyone's story: the courtship, the marriage, the Brooklyn tenement, the twenty-hour workdays during the war, one daughter, another daughter, a contract to tool rifle butts for the U.S. Army, his wood shop moving to Orchard Street. The family would move up to Bayside, Queens, a house off Horace Harding Boulevard, a smooth, sturdy brick house on Two Hundred and Second Street. And with the whole wheeling world in front of them, the war over, the business established, the girls, the house, everything having come true for them, the man would die.

Snowstorm, shoveling, front door standing open, fresh burn of cold, their father on the floor in the bedroom, girls all eyes as they sat with their coloring books, their mother accidentally kicking the crayon box, the scar from the cut on Anna's leg like a little proof, a souvenir she kept her whole life.

Their mother would lose the business, the car, the house in Bayside—her husband dying with all of their dreams, but without her—and back down in the world, back down to Brooklyn, to Greenpoint, to Calyer Street, idle nights of the ring, the woman spinning it like a quarter on the kitchen table.

She'd call the girls to sit with her, ask them if they remembered the story of the ring. Anna would watch the grim set of her down-turned mouth. And Jean would say, Yes, yes, we remember. And then she'd ask practical questions. Can we go outside, Mom? We'll stay on the street?

Sundays, their mother walked the mile north to Calvary Cemetery, in Queens, to hold the hard cold hands of angels, pet their wings, smooth their nightgowns made of stone. She placed pebbles at the feet of one angel to mark her visits—a statue standing near his stone—his own grave a modest gray granite, her own name engraved below his. It was pure melodrama, she knew, but still she removed her ring and climbed onto the girl's pedestal, hid the ring behind the angel's collarbone, in the depression where rain collected.

Then she would walk.

A small, dark figure on these mornings, she weaved the hills of the cemetery, her trail in the silver-wet grass between the many crosses and crypts and trees. That undersea quiet of cemetery, and the small brick church, Saint Callixtus, sold flowers and vigil candles, the candles flickering in little red glasses, the money always untended. She lit the long wooden match off another flame. Then she moved into the vaulted quiet of the church to pray, though she never really prayed. She never came here to mourn or grieve or pray or anything, except be alone and quiet, take her ring and give it to an angel, traipse free over the grave-crowded hills.

On her return back down to the world again, she walked the low drawbridge over the Newtown Creek between Brooklyn and Queens, the water all curdled with sewage and colorful rings of oil. She stood at the rail and saw that mother on the ship, that small white bundle of blankets in her arms.

Almost as an afterthought, she could add the wind coming cool off the bow, add the barest hints of burning coal in the air, the watchful rows of rivets along the side of the boat, the skin of the ocean alive as an animal, all these little details to make it true, to make it happen just as she remembered it, that one graceful moment when the woman curled herself over the rail of the ship, Joseph saying how he'd not have been surprised if, when the boat had moved on, he'd seen her trying to stand on the unsure surface of the waves, such was the tension of the sea that night.

LIKE A DEMON

Two of them in a diner off the highway, booth by a window, poor woman trying to smile it all nice—nice in a way it never was, nice in a way it always was—mother trying to just never mind her son, just ignore this strange person, pay no attention as he lifts his shirt slightly, black handle of a .45 tucked into his pants, gun exactly where he promised it would be.

Now, she says, of all the stupid things.

You would know, he tells her—and he can't seem to get that grin off his face—and he looks away to the traffic, sunlight, strip mall in the distance, whole world so bright and oblivious, waitress clearing dishes from the tables oblivious, cook behind counter in his apron oblivious, slushy sound of cutlery and voices, walls of quilted aluminum, and his mother staring at him all the while. Could out-patience a statue, woman with heating elements for eyes, that tungsten glow on the side of his face until he turns to his mother, finally, her hand out over the table to him.

May I? she asks — and she tips her head to one side — and he gently places the gun in her palm without a word.

It's warm, she says. And heavy, much heavier than I'd have expected.

She weighs the pistol in her palm. Something unreal to this, her fingers fitting the grip, the trigger guard, the trigger. He watches and leans forward to narrate what she's holding — Colt Commander, M-1911, single-action, semiautomatic, standard-issue blah, blah, blah — as if he really knew what he was talking about, his mother's eyes snaking across the diner, gun pointing at the waitress, waitress suddenly backing away slow, sandwich platters balanced on her arms, entire place going airless and hushed, everything turning ridiculous, son tucking a few dollars next to his plate, saying, C'mon, Mom, let's get going.

Underhum of tires on highway, bright blue wash of sunshine, and the clean getaway of Lincoln floating big and loose on the road, woman's little dog on her lap, mother holding gun like a bird in her hand. Probably just the speed that makes it shake like that, pistol nervous and shivering with her holding it. A tree, a barn, a police car on the side of the road — miles turning into minutes, minutes into miles — and he glances every so often at her, the gun in her hand, his mother's knuckles like chicken bones, the dog across her legs.

So, he says, any chance I can grab that thing back from you now?

And his mother turns to him, stares as if not quite able to place this stranger, her mouth going all seasick, something helpless and pleading about her eyes, as if she's on the verge

112

of saying, I'm sorry, who are you? And why are you driving my car? Where are you taking us?

You okay over there, Mom?

She presses her lips to a line and raises the empty point of the gun to the side of his chest. You know, she says, I have such an incredible urge to shoot you.

Better let me pull over first, he tells her—and he goes all cheery and nonchalant and proceeds to ease off the next exit—and he rides them beyond the gas station, beyond the transfer station, pulls into the sandy clearing in the distance, where he says she can roll his body into the tall grass. His mother just sits in the passenger seat, not moving, not opening the door. She just watches as he wades into the grass, his mother waiting as he stands in front of the car, her son with his arms raised, that gunpoint smile on his face. Well? he calls to her—and he opens his arms, offers his chest, closes his eyes, but nothing happens, his mother a silhouette with that dog on her lap.

There's an electricity of insects from the brush, and the son breathes deep and circles around to his side of the car, continues to the back fender, opens his pants and pisses into the grass, his legs heavy as he gets behind the wheel again. Not going to happen, he says, is it?

What's that? she asks.

You're not going to shoot me, are you?

She shakes her head no. Sorry.

Big fat breeze of car halfway through New York State, halfway to Michigan, road like a wire in front of them, and his mother places the gun on the seat, saying to do whatever he wants with it, saying she doesn't care. She turns to watch the rain approach, wipers beating back and forth, tires on the road like a hiss of steam, blind spray of trucks to pass. The dog never takes its eyes off the son, the son taking the pistol from the seat and carefully leaning across to close the gun in the glove compartment.

Halfway through Ohio, and she rests her eyes, her face all pinches and pulls of clay, that quiet scrape of her breathing as she falls asleep. Another hour, and Michigan, and he talks to his father in his mind—goes back and forth with the man—son trying to tell all these things to the man. Like the mystery of the gun he can't explain. And why he wanted to take her to visit in the first place. None of it making any sense to him, starting with his father and mother eloping all those years ago.

No one sets out to be a complete fuckup, as his father once told him. It just sort of happens, Michael. (Note to self: Your father uses your name over the phone and safe bet he's trying to impart some bit of wisdom he feels you need to know, some lesson he believes his duty to teach to you. Either that or he's loaded again. Have to listen for those wind chimes of ice in his drink, man all homesick and goosey on the line, your poor old man asking if you remember some song he used to sing to you and your brother when you were kids, and you just waiting for the right moment to hit him up for some money, just waiting to stick him with some last-minute knife, asking if somebody diddled them as kids or something, asking how else could he explain why everyone's so fucked up in this family.)

Almost dark when they stop for gas, his mother asleep, his hand going to her hand, the dog always watching him. His mother's skin is dry as paper, and he cups his palm on her fist until she wakes. Not used to this kind of touch, and she startles. What's wrong? We there already?

Everything's fine, Mom. Almost there.

It's dark, road clear and dry, a few more miles and he's thinking again of his father — time he and Charlie went to visit the man — the brothers sent to see their father in the summer, two of them nine or ten years old, their mother putting them on a train in Providence, their father waiting on a platform in Detroit, shirt pressed and pants creased for the occasion, his boots with zippers up the inside ankles, the boys following that hard click of heels to the car. Impala floats wide and loose as a motorboat in the dusk, streetlights and traffic out of the city, that radial drone of road under everything. Soon they're having burgers and malts in Flint, stopping at a gas station in Saginaw, and then another hour to Grayling, Portage Lake, and the cottage.

A lifetime ago already — twenty, twenty-five, try more than thirty years since any of this — yet it truly *is* like yesterday, three of them on that big bench seat of his car, windows open with cool pour of air, hum of roadway and radio, man with his arm straight, wrist flexed over wheel, cigarette after cigarette as he drives. And this little kid — young ver-

115

sion of himself—he watches as the boy picks the plastic tubing of the armrest, as he fingers the metal cover of the ashtray, as he glances to his father's face in that green glow of dash, the man's reflection like a ghost in the windshield, he and his brother memorizing the man, neither of them realizing how much they miss their father, how much they will have to stay loyal to their mother, how quiet and guarded and less sure of everything they will become, their father more present when he's gone, their mother less home when she's there, the boys holding their breath at night along with the house.

You know the kind of house. Can see the doilies, the photos, all the little efforts she makes, porcelain collies on the shelf, all the bric-a-brac of hope, two kids listening to the way she cries at night, the sound like water pouring down the walls, the sound like birds nesting in the attic, the sound of her crying becoming nothing like crying at all, as if they might have been mistaken right along, can't trust their own ears, their mother maybe laughing to herself below them, woman giggling over some secret joy she's been saving, some kind of happiness she's holding until they're old enough to appreciate it, until they're ready to take care of whatever it is she will someday give them.

At least this is what he and Charlie tell each other.

And his brother asks, When will we be big enough?

I don't know, Charlie. Seventh grade maybe. Or high school.

And there are silences so loud he can still hear them now, all these years later. Driving along on a highway, for instance, and he still feels that strange sense of pressure in the walls as the bedroom sinks deeper and deeper into night, can still listen to Charlie breathing himself to sleep, the moon in the dormer window, that dust of moonlight over everything, trees swaying with the wind, and his father always pale and transparent at the window, the man always staring from the other side of the glass. Even if his father isn't there, the man is still there somehow, windowed away from them, standing mute and drowned in the light.

These dreams are fists. They are hard and closed and never will you open them, though they are yours and yours alone to open. Who else would want them, really? Who else would care?

Someone says you'll never do a certain thing, never become this person you say you'll be, never be this untangler, this undoer, this beautiful little dreamer, this lying little sneak, someone says you'll never change, you'll never bring these two worlds together, but then just watch — and *voilà!* — you're back at the cottage again, opening the car door for your mother, your father there on the porch waiting, hellos and hugs and everyone into the living room, cold can of beer in your hand like magic, chitchat about the drive as you stretch your shoulders, your mother's little dog crying to go outside, you offering to run this chore for them, your mother and father alone inside together, you and the dog out in the yard.

Be so easy if the gun felt natural. So simple to just drift toward the Lincoln, that mineral pull of pistol from the glove compartment, imagine it warm and heavy, picture yourself decisive and clear for once in your life. Yet that's not the way this works for you—sorry—you might yearn for a bullet, might wish for some sharp demon of pain burning like a wick, but you must not yearn enough to become wild and ruthless and real like that. Instead you tug your brother dog by the leash, grass wet and cold, saying, Pay attention, saying, Just do your business already, saying, Let's wait on the steps like good kids for a little while.

Let them have some time in the cottage, you say, your mother and father, one last hurrah for them. Remember she once told you that they made love on these visits, woman saying how she and your father would be together while you and your brother played in the yard. And what does one do with a detail like that? No wonder they don't lie still in your mind, your parents, this life never anything like you expect it to be.

Can feel your mother and father telegraphed in the wood floor as you sit on the porch with the dog. Her footsteps in the house, his voice like mice running inside the walls. That cool of the lake seeps in, that taffeta of air through the leaves of trees, and you wait for that knock and scuff of the screen door opening behind you, as it will, you're sure, your mother out under the porch light, your father right behind her, two of them wondering what happened to you? Are you still out here?

And are they talking to you or the dog? Not easy to tell. Either way, you both tip your heads as they approach, their voices all singsong, like they're trying to catch you and tame you and show you how they must love you again.

THE OLD WOMAN AND HER THIEF

On her deathbed, as she drew what were to be her last breaths on God's green earth, the old woman made a confession so terrible to her husband that—even under circumstances as solemn and sorrowful as these—he could hardly take the secret as true, let alone forgive her for it. He listened by her side, as if struck dumb by a club, and when she pressed her lips tight against admitting anything more and a silence had passed, a long silence in which she could hear herself swallow away the taste of coins in her mouth, just when she expected the final lifting of the veil to all her life's meaning, the old man hiccupped.

It might have been the fever in her mind, but she could not accept this as her life's reward, and she lay there and blinked her eyes and half expected her husband to cough up an olive pit or cherry stone. She watched for his lips to purse and spit an inky seed into her hand, but only the startle of his hiccups came, haphazard and loud in the room. She could feel each jump through the bedsprings to her, and finally she asked him to go drink some seltzer water and stand on his head and let her die. She lay flat and let her eyes close to the dim room and tried to savor the slow lift and release of each breath in her chest, and on into the night she lay at rest and at peace like this.

But she did not die.

Contrary to all they had expected and provided for, in three days' time the old woman was sitting up in bed and answering her mail. Scattered about her lay books and dishes and flower arrangements, bowls of ripened fruit, her little radio and reading lamp. The curtains and windows were opened wide. And on the morning of the fourth day the doctor clicked his tongue and pronounced, almost begrudgingly, that she was quite recovered. The undertaker arrived to roll the casket and wreaths out of the old couple's parlor, where she was to be laid out, and the man's cologne lingered so long after him in the room that her husband lit matches to kill the scent.

Improbable as it became, in two more days the old woman's appetite for chocolate and red wine returned. And her husband knew she was truly well when she asked for a pot of coffee and a bundt cake. As he ventured to the bakery, he caught himself whistling—it was a brilliant spring morning, after all, and he breathed in the cool air and stopped to look out over the hills in the distance, clouds driven across the sky by the blue clear winds, all the trees in leaf and flower, and the traffic of people out walking and working, the report of hammers and whine of saws, the spring birds on the grass, the grass in the sun the color of old yellowed silver—and on he went walking for her cake, the thought dawning on him that soon she would be up and off to the market herself, lunching with friends, shopping for groceries, everything just like usual. Her Tuesday bridge ladies, her Thursday museum committee, her Friday reading to the blind.

The old man's heart became divided after his wife's had almost been carried off. On the one side, all his prayers had been answered: his wife alive, their world restored, and the warm sun of another spring upon them both. What more could he ask for? And yet, in ways he couldn't help, her confession about her thief lay heavy on the other side of his heart. And this half of him grew heavier as the days passed. He began to fancy that he had somehow been tricked by life, a thing he had never before thought possible.

Perhaps as a consequence of this division in his heart, or as a result of the wear of his wife's illness upon him, or even the peculiar strain of her growing wellness upon him, or perhaps the gout in his ankles when it rained, or the ceaseless passing of friends and family and whole ways of life, or perhaps just the troubled rags of feeling old and dull to the world. Whatever the reason, all the things in his life grew increasingly strange to the old man. He would glimpse — or would think he had glimpsed — fruit bats hanging folded with the coats in the closet, turtles in place of pillows on the couch. A pair of boots became muskrats under the bench in the hall, and then they were dachshunds, and then, a step closer, they were boots again.

As the days passed, the old man went around braced against the world. He didn't know if he believed what he saw or saw what he believed. Was it what you saw or what you thought you saw? Did you only see what you expected to see? Didn't know anything the way he used to know—or didn't know anything the way he *thought* he'd known—and it exhausted him to chase his tail like this. He often went to lie down on the day bed and close his eyes for fear that the truth would be revealed to him. He didn't trust his heart could take it.

On the face of it, the man and his wife seemed the darlings of destiny, not so much the envy of the little valley town as its collective hope. You'd have to be blind not to see the care and craft of the old man's silver shop, just as you'd have to be heartless not to find the woman's reprieve from death to be nothing short of miraculous, not to assume it meant she had purposes unfinished in the town, not to be moved when you saw her approach with a bundle of flowers in her arms. Despite her years and her children all far-flung, who wouldn't stop her in the street and say—among the many things people said—that the old woman appeared more radiant and unshakable than ever? Who wouldn't hold the woman at arm's length and tell her how glad they were to hear there'd be no funeral?

Truth is, she'd say, I never felt better, never felt more—dare I even say it?—more *sprightly*.

Yes, they'd say, wasn't *sprightly* exactly how she looked? And they'd hold her hands and tell how they wept for joy to learn of her recovering, the old woman smiling and throwing back her head, brimming with all the giddy pleasure of a schoolgirl.

Oh, I feel I've been gone so long, she'd say. Come sit and tell me how you've been all this time.

They'd sit to tea in the sleepy shade of the market trees, she and her friends, that drift of carnival music from the organ grinder, to whom she read on Fridays, that swift little squirrel monkey of his tumbling through the square with the jangling pouch of dimes and nickels. Everything was just like usual—nearly everything restored—the pranks of the monkey, the storm crabs in cages for sale, the ice and fish and roasting nuts and seeds, the smell of burnt sugar and salt, the warm coins in her one hand ready to give to the laughing monkey, her wallet clutched tight in the other, because she knew how the monkey too was a thief.

Home from the market she walked with her basket of greens and bread and cheese, a newspaper packet of sunflower seeds and a bottle of red wine, as well as the notion to tell her husband all the household scandals she'd heard, all the antics of the monkey she'd watched, how the animal would sneak his tail around a little boy and tip the boy's cap over his eyes. And as she went toward home she watched the sky for stray birds, hoped for him to return, the old woman always hoping for her old lost-to-the-world Romeo.

The sun settled behind the trees, and she stopped in a small garden park and set down her basket and rubbed the aches out of her hands. In the fountain a copper goose spit water up over its head onto its back. She waited and watched the sunlit fingers of the highest tree branches. And softly she whistled and said his name, rustled the seeds against the newspaper, and again more boldly she called to him.

The air went powdery toward dusk, and she heard the slow ring of the vesper bell, and still no Romeo. She knew better than to hope, but each stir of shadow in the damp air made her turn and call his name and see and know, despite her best hopes, that her thief was not there.

If it came back at all, the old couple's history came back to them like a story they'd heard about or read about somewhere long ago, their memories scarcely their own anymore, their life like a nursery rhyme. Once upon a time and the old man — a young man then, of course, still sticky with the things he touched in life — stumbled upon a bird's nest in the woods near his home. In the leaves nearby lay a crow, black and folded closed, its feet cut off.

These days were days of great superstition, days when farmers poisoned cribs of corn to feed migrating birds, birds thought to bring disease and other sorrows, birds believed to be omens of famine and death, birds always associated with misfortune. For many years one could pay one's taxes with salted owl's eyes and crow's feet. Springtime brought festivals to little towns in the valley. Cannons shot nets over fields of birds, the birds lured with corn seed, the children running to club the struggling creatures with broom handles. Many birds grew skittish over the years and learned not to sing. Fewer and fewer returned each season, until fowling parties combed the woods to shake and chop a final nest or two from the trees. All that remained of some species — the scarlet hurry hawk, the tiny skittlelink — were a few sun-faded specimens under the smudged glass of museum cabinets, a bronze nameplate, a detail about habitat or mating.

And once upon a time, the old man—still a young man then—he came across that crow lying broken like an umbrella in the woods, that perfect circle of twigs and sticks a few yards away, that glint of tinsel in the cup of grass. And whenever he thought back to this moment, he'd see himself staring at the egg in the hold of the nest, the surface of this egg as smooth and perfect as a moon opal.

He'd remember not a speck of sound disturbing the woods, the quiet columns of trees, the pools of light on the path, the light falling as snow falls when there is no wind, everything hushed. And when, as from a dream, the man stepped forward and removed his sweater and stooped to wrap the nest, he heard leaves rustle above him. As he carried the nest back through the woods, carried it like a boy carries a bowl full of soup, he hoped to high heaven that his young bride at home would know what to do with a miracle such as this.

Hatch and raise him—was it ever really a question?—a silk-black crow toddling about the rooms of their house. They fed him and kept him safe—the bird so perfectly black he moved like oil—taught him to speak and fly, showed him how to eat at the dinner table. He learned to waltz, their orphan Romeo, learned to purr and bark and howl to the moon. In the parlor at night the man showed their crow how to sing like the nightingale, like the chaffinch, like the sparrow, like the gentle playing of the late-night radio, the piano and soprano so like birds themselves. And with her knitting halted in her lap, the old woman—a young woman then, of course, still undisappointed by life—she'd watch the crow on her husband's knee, watch Romeo singing so eager to the man, watch the bird's feet grabbing at the man's trousers, her husband's eyes closed and head tilted, the bird like a violin, the bird like a cello, the bird like a piano again, its eyes shining like onyx under the light, the crow turning back and forth from him to her, her to him, as if they were tossing something across the room between them.

And in the mornings, the man arose and readied himself for the silver shop—where day after day he hammered the town hallmark into piles of knives and forks and spoons, so many clattering spoons, you'd have never imagined enough mouths for all of them—Romeo flying alongside as he walked the road to work. After the bird hurried home to the woman, she would tidy the house and chatter on to her Romeo in what would start as gladness and would amount, in the end, to a steady slow pour of loneliness.

By the time their children arrived—two boys, two girls, each a year apart—and by the time the children were half grown and half out the door and married and moved away, many things had come to pass in the couple's life together, many things in what had seemed to the woman just a heap of idle days, days scarcely strung along together, not a thing appearing to happen or change or move. Time felt like the thinnest of strings, no end to hold, the beads of days sliding clean off as if they had never been. Or as if they had always been, days both fleeting and eternal at the same time, this paradox nearly impossible for her, time being something entirely different from her experience of it.

Just as sure as the sun crossed the day, the old man wet his head every morning and walked to his work, the sterling bowls and pitchers and loud piles of endless cutlery. And each morning Romeo flew along with him and perched from tree to tree and sang the songs of the whippoorwill, the bullfinch, the yellow forktail, the bluebird, the naked-throated robbybell, the songs of the whiskey-jack, and the waxwing, the waxbill, and as the man unlocked the door of his shop, Romeo perched atop the roof's peak and sang his catalogue of night lieder from the radio, the bird hollering out like a ringing telephone and a lawn-mower engine to make the man laugh.

He waited for the first sweet whiffs of coal smoke from the chimney, and then the crow started home over the town, flew with an eye for things to steal as he returned to the woman, who sat watching for him on the porch, the children off to school, her coffee and cake nearly finished.

She scanned the horizon of trees for his wind-tossed silhouette flying safely home—the bird like a shadow—his eyes shining for that glint of gold to bring home to her, the woman waiting to hear those wings hissing as he flew close, the woman eager to catch that gold chain dangling in his beak, the woman hoping for another of the many gifts he carried home to her out of love. Always he would come to the porch and walk his nodding walk, his toes clicking on the wood. He would bow for her to scratch the nape of his neck and rub his feathers against the grain, as he so loved her to do. And when she reached out her hand to him, palm up, Romeo would open his beak and place into the cup of her hand a child's jack, or a bullet shell, or a long necklace of pearls with a gold hasp, a heavy brass plumb bob, a pair of golden mustache scissors . . .

Each became a gift picked special for her, the best of these objects setting into motion whole machines of scandal and gossip, the old woman carrying home the stories to her husband from the market each week. Such as the rumor of the missing gypsy pendant, said to be a nail from the True Cross, the gypsies leaving a curse that would scatter all the town's children far from home. The story of the careless heart locket, its loss undoing two young lovers, their families feuding over the millpond, the pond soon to be poisoned by the tannery. And there was the pair of platinum-rimmed eyeglasses, stolen from the jeweler, the man stumbling to his death out the open window of his studio, that scatter of uncut diamonds cast around his body in such a way that people said the jeweler had become, through long practice and labor, the very stuff of his art. In the weeks that followed the jeweler's demise, children would throw stones at the glass blower to see if he shattered, the banker would snip off his little finger with a cigar cutter, and the old goldsmith in a neighboring village would be found bound to a tree in the woods, his veins opened and his blood supposedly cast into coins. The town never did rise above its shame to breathe a word about the fate of the quiet vintner, Lord rest his soul.

Many years passed this way—the town secrets tied to a

crow and a thin old woman—and anonymously she parceled her hoard to the museum and library and church charities. She gave to the organ grinder and quietly stirred silver brooches and rings into her husband's foundry pots, which cooked forever in the center chimney of his shop. And though she wanted only to tell her husband the real secrets beneath the secrets she brought home from the market, she didn't know how to explain so he would understand.

And after all the years had passed, after Romeo's feathers had gone lusterless and dusty gray, even after he hardly toddled out of his cage to her hand, she would reach to his perch and pet his face to say good night, Romeo purring to her in the voices of her children, in the sighs and coughs of her husband, in the familiar squawk of the kitchen door being opened and closed, her own voice coming out of his dry beak, the crow whispering her back to herself, Yes, pretty bird.

And she would smile and whisper to him, Yes.

And they would try to soothe each other, saying, Yes, yes, yes, yes.

When she'd first taken ill, the children came home with their spouses and children, but soon they begged off and returned to jobs in cities scattered far away. Their presence only served to remind the old man of their absence, and he thought it funny none of them had wondered about Romeo, the bird practically a brother to the children. The old man thought he heard the crow return to the window in the tapping of a branch. He thought how sad and alone he was, none of their children becoming a friend to them, he and his wife passing their years with apprentices, with bridge ladies, with nothing in the end but work and Romeo and each other.

He didn't do anything with this sadness—unless allowing it to wash over him was doing something—unless wandering through the woods with packets of seeds counted for something. He feared the crow dead and whistled up to the trees and looked for Romeo's crushed bones and feathers among the ferns and the wood-roses, the woods holding quiet around him, the clouds in the sky through the leaves far above like the breaking surface of the sea. Again that swell of sadness and sympathy—for the birds, for his wife, for Romeo, for his friend the vintner, for all the sufferings of the little town, and for his own self, the old man with his hunched-over life of silver and chasing tools—and he could almost feel the weight of the crow landing on him, that unmistakable weight of Romeo standing on his arm, the bird light in the way that a bird is light yet solid, the old man singing night songs to the trees until his throat was red, the old man trying to call the crow home for her.

No Romeo came to him, and with his boots wet through from pushing aside the morning ferns, the old man started home, and a flash caught his eye, a baby's bracelet. He brushed the dirt from it and hurried home all full of pride—the man sticky as pine pitch again with life—smiling to hold the little prize out to his wife. She would fly to him, he thought, her eyes all alight for him. But instead she screamed so fiercely that he thought she was in pain and dying all over again. She clutched at the bracelet, and he tried to cover her with blankets, tried to calm her, the man patting the blankets as if putting out a fire. What have you done with him? she cried, her face tight and scoured-looking. What have you done? Where is he? Where is Romeo?

Her voice so hard, her words so angry, the realization falling on him like a mallet, and the old man stuttered that he didn't do anything to him, didn't touch the bird, didn't even see him anywhere. The old man tried saying how, in the woods, by chance, he'd found the bracelet under a fern, with other ferns. He pointed to the toes of his boots, as if offering more proof, and took mushrooms from his coat pockets and cupped them in his hand to show her. He held out a tiny pinecone from his breast pocket, the man desperate as a crow to quiet and comfort her.

She looked at his feet, the brown boots dark with wet, and she lay back heavily and brought the gold metal to her face, touched it to her lips, touched it to her tongue, and tried to catch that humid smell of Romeo on the bracelet. She didn't look to her husband, even when he sat down beside her on the bed and took her hand, and toward his weight she tipped slightly and poured out even more of her life's confession to him, told of the thief, the locket, the jewelry maker's glasses.

The old man would go to his grave wondering what more he could have asked for: his wife recovered, their world spared, spring upon them. And yet, as the days passed, he found himself unable to be roused from bed, unable to venture far from the house, and many mornings he would lie in bed, staring at the window, his mind flitting in and out of dreams and memories, the difference between the two no longer important for him.

What's more, the old woman had become well with a vengeance. Her appetites restored and habits renewed, she went out each day and bounced as she stepped down the sidewalk into town. The old man watched her go, her white hair shining in the sun. And he watched, and kept watching, the empty street. A little breeze came in the window, and the curtains rose up and bowed down slow before him. And when the old man stepped outside into the light, he thought diamond necklaces hung on the wet grass. Or had the house windows shattered? Or could the dew be stars in the lawn?

Stand up straight, old man, he said to himself. Enough is enough is enough already.

And he would turn from where he stood and go back inside to lie down on the day bed and look at his dry spotted hands until he had chased himself inside-out. He looked through the window and curtains and was back to watching as the sun—the sun with all the patience and fortitude of the mountain and woods—the sun doing its work of turning the shadows of the lampposts up on their ends, of holding those shadows there, and then of gently laying the shadows out long again opposite. And dusk brought the vesper bells and the approaching click of his wife's heels on the walk, the heavy creak of her basket filled with dinner greens and fruit, the old man's heart chanting that the trouble's no trouble, the trouble's no trouble, the trouble's no trouble . . .

And over dinner and wine he listened as she chatted cards

and told how, in the market, the monkey stole a ball from a boy, and how last week she read a pirate story to the organ grinder, and how she could swear the monkey was weeping when the parrot in the story is captured by mutineers and is made to give evidence against his captain.

In the living room, late into the night, the old silversmith and his wife would sit and listen to the radio. Sometimes they'd remember the past for each other — their marriage trees as saplings, their trip to Spain — but mostly they just remained quiet together in the room, the man absently paging through a book of paintings, a book of flowers, a book of children's stories, and the woman's knitting halted on her lap as she stared at the dark empty windows, the soprano on the radio rising onto her toes, her piano slowly falling to the floor — and coming to rest — like a leaf.

You know who'd have liked that song? he asked her.

The needles in her hands began to tick together up and down again, and she looked over at his finger running along the edge of a page, and when she raised her eyes to his, he winked. She dropped a stitch and pulled out lengths of yarn from the skein tumbling on the floor.

After the next song — a waltz that had been popular when they were courting — she said that that wasn't so bad, either, was it?

Incredible, said the man. He hummed and closed the book on his lap and watched as she knit. He laid aside the book. Know what I'd most like to be in my next life?

What's that?

A musician, he said, and learn to play like that.

I'll see what I can do, she told him.

He sat down. He had been sitting all along, but he sat down even more, as though forcing air from his body to touch bottom with something. He sat heavy in his old bones and looked at her. He had been looking at her all along, all his life he had been looking, but he looked even more — and she was a wolf with knitting in her lap, then she was a little girl frail and lost in gray hair and old lady clothes, her knuckles swollen, and then, again, what was she, old man? Who was she besides the only one you'd ever love in this life of clattersome spoons and singing crows? A smile floated to his face all by itself, he could feel it rising in his cheeks and eyes, this brightening, and he found a laugh starting deep out of him, and soon he was laughing in that big easy way some men have, men of the moment who can shake off their troubles and let out that three-cheers-to-the-fiddle-player laugh, which rattles bottles against barroom mirrors.

When she started to say something, he rose to his feet and took her hand and led her out to the porch, where they stood together and watched the night, the black trees, the moon, the stars so close you could stir them with a finger, the rustle of an animal in the leaves under the porch. And they closed up the house and went to bed, it being late, but the man had a tickle in his throat and couldn't sleep in the quiet and began coughing. He got up and went to the kitchen for seltzer water and lemon. In the silvery moondark he sat at the kitchen table and cleaned his teeth with a toothpick.

That morning — the sunlight streaming into the house through the curtains, the birds outside singing — when she went to the room with the day bed, she carried a tray with their coffee and juice and muffins to him and found that, during the night, the old man had died.

There was consolation in the busy details of the wake and funeral, in the playing of host to friends and family, in the attending to train schedules and sleeping arrangements. An odd, quiet solace also crept into the old woman's answering of sympathy cards and her writing of money orders to the churchyard and stone carver and undertaker, that cologne of his carrying the memory of every death in town. And at every other corner someone waited to keep her distracted with lunch in the market, with idle whiffs of gossip, with invitations to dinner. It struck her that everyone — in a fit of pity — conspired to let her never be alone.

She had her bridge ladies, her museum committee, her Friday reading to the blind, the organ grinder with his cream-clotted eyes, his little-man monkey over his shoulder, the old woman sometimes wondering if the man was even listening. It seemed he showed interest only when she stopped or digressed from the story they were reading.

What's wrong? he'd ask. Why'd you stop?

Or, Excuse me, he'd say, but it says that for real?

Or, Keep going, please!

She would smile over to the monkey — the animal crouched so attentive in his little mustard-colored suit — and back to the page she'd return, clear her throat, the old widow picking up from where she'd broken off. The man wanted only ghost stories, of late. And the more avenging the justice, the more haunted the conscience, the better. And the monkey would snort at each turn of events, at each squeaking door and midnight romp he would somersault in his seat, and a dull guilt would tie up the old woman's neck, as if her reading held within it something mildly illicit. With the bright morning and the chirping birds, the stories of grave robbers or shipwrecks seemed to her like brandy at breakfast.

But to see the monkey squirm in his seat, to have him begin to clap as she reached lunchtime, to have him pulling his hair as the ghosts all marched onto the waves to their foggy ships, that was fine for her. And as the monkey chortled and squeaked, the organ grinder opened his onion-white eyes. Bravo! he said. Bravo!

Encore! Encore!

And she whiled away the afternoon with lunch and coffee and the sweet organ music in the market, the crabs and roasting seeds and fruit stalls, and the same water-cool shade of the trees, the same benches where she sat and met the usual passersby. And closer to evening, the old woman sat out on the porch with her wine and chocolate, the sun sinking behind the trees, the branches in strong tangled shadow. It was autumn but the light was warm and she waited for night to fall as birds flew home to their nests. She carried sunflower seeds out of habit, but she hardly ever watched for her Romeo and his soft return anymore, which she had once seen in her mind so clearly, a smudge of black against the horizon, his raucous flying home so fully imagined that it seemed to her already accomplished. The roll of his wings, the fanned spread of his tail, the silky hiss of his feathers, the tick of his feet upon the wood porch.

Hello, little bird, she said to a grackle in the shrub, the bird tipping its head and looking to the seeds she held out to him in her hand.

She told him to take some, her voice looping high and low, the bird squeaking out a rusty gate of a song, flitting to a branch in a tree, slightly higher than before. The old woman stood and came forward again with her hand out. When she was close enough to see how his eye shone yellow, how his black feathers glossed purple, she watched him whet his beak on the branch and flutter to a tree near the street and turn on his perch and watch her again, the bird saying to follow him.

She was on the sidewalk and past the post office and fire station and market, her bird before her in the tree just distant, past houses and smells of dinner, past the cemetery and church. Tree by tree she followed until they were far beyond even the railway station, and suddenly the little grackle was gone.

The sky darkened left to right over the town, the moon also was starting to rise nearly full, bright and clear and pale enough to cast shadows. And into the gutter the old woman pitched the seeds in her hand. Beyond the closed market stalls, she could see the glow of lights against the museum façade. Every light in the palace of the museum must have been on—whole place alive with light—but not a soul stood on the steps at the entrance as she approached, no guard or coat-check with his arm draped over the ancient lion in the foyer.

Music, yes, and the muddled drone of voices and glassware from the ballroom, like some empty and haunted ship, the old woman feeling invisible as she turned at the suits of armor down the long side hall, draped ceiling to floor with royal tapestries, the music and voices fading behind her, only the occasional burst of girls' laughter flying after her.

At the end of the hall the huge double doors with porthole windows stood dark, and when she pushed the doors all their heaviness swung easily and silently aside and opened onto her favorite of all rooms in the museum. The doors closed behind her and she let her eyes adjust to the dim light. All was quiet and still, that tinwork of blood she could hear in her ears. And slow and gradual, the sponged clouds came clear on the high-domed ceiling, and once more she was in the company of the twelve-month gulls and blue kestrels that flew suspended on strings above her, and the huge albatross wandering there along its wires above her.

She walked beneath them—the big wheeling birds under clouds—moved to the wall of bright cases, each holding a bird as posed and half-real as a painting of a bird under glass. A diorama of passenger pigeons, each of them staring with glass-bead eyes at the room, their eggs speckled like stones. And next to the pigeons, as remote as the rest, the bourbon crested starling sat on a branch, holding a plastic cricket in his beak, accounts telling how this bird could be batted down with a yardstick, poor creatures so trusting and tame and delicious. And the old woman came to the great auk and could practically hear him call his own name, his feathers soft as velvet, his tiny swimming wings spread, the old woman's hand next to the glass as if he might be frightened away at any moment. She passed a collection of finches, the birds so delicate and alert that she had to remind herself that they were hollow inside. The spectacled cormorant, the Chatman Island rail, the wood pigeon, the society parakeet, all of these birds sitting stuffed and staged and dead to the world.

And at the end of the room, at the window, the old woman caught herself reflected in the glass and reached up and turned the metal lock on the sash and lifted open the window, the weights in the walls banging, the night dark outside, the air cool, the sounds again of a party, the streetlamp of a moon above. And what was so wrong with admitting it, admitting that she would love to fly home right now like a bird? That she would have given anything to go dark through the black air, instead of having to walk past the tuxedoed thick-wits splashing in the fountain, the bare-shouldered women giggling as they held the men's empty shoes in their arms. That insolent look of the night guard back on duty, his feet up on the desk, that look enough to crush her, enough to make her feel small and lonely, lonely for her life when it was as yet undiminished, when it was still there in front of them, when life was not these vanishing wings behind her.

She walked home cold under the moon—which had two blue rings around it, meaning frost before morning—and she was home again, her red wine where she had left it on the porch, next to the chocolate and fruit. She took everything inside and sat in her chair and hugged herself with a heavy shawl until her teeth unclenched from the cold. She stared at the room, the fireplace, the radio, the rug, her husband's empty chair, her basket of tangled yarn. And she didn't know, in the end, how to sit without hope, how to sit without wishing for his return, for her Romeo to open his beak and place a necklace in her palm, for this old gone bird to return to her, for him to bring back all the many voices she had grown so lonesome for.

She heard the rumble of a train running through town, and then all was quiet again. She raised her palm to her mouth to taste the salt from the sunflower seeds, and she heard mice in the walls. Far away a dog barked. And she must have started to sleep in her chair, for she was awakened by scratching in the kitchen. She feared the mice had become rats, their clawing so persistent that she took the iron poker from the fireplace. She turned on the light, and the noise stopped. At the counter she checked that the flour and sugar jars were closed, and when she turned to leave, the scratching like tapping began again.

Then at the back door, his hand on the screen—she caught the little gray face in the bottom corner—the organ grinder's monkey in his mustard-colored suit. She smiled and let him in. My, my, she said, what a nice surprise!

And the monkey climbed up on the counter and held out his hand to shake.

And what brings you here, you little rascal?

The monkey's smile widened as he went across to the table and sat down, his tail coiled around the chair back. He crossed his legs like a gentleman, pretended to smoke a cigarette.

Well then, she said, may I offer something to eat?

She set the table and began putting out cheese and crackers and nuts, a tiny bowl of olives, some fruit and wine, and the monkey nibbled at a pretzel. He never took his eyes from her. And when she sat down, she offered him chocolate and began talking. It's like a tea party, she said, telling him what amounted to a long pour of days and once-upon-a-time memories, the monkey listening rapt, like it was a story, her voice stopping only long enough to refill a glass or crack a nut for her little friend.

Then, in the distance, they heard the voice of the organ grinder up the street. Arch-ie! he called, his voice breaking and raw. Don't do this, he yelled. Come home, please.

Neither the monkey nor the woman moved. They stared at each other, and the man passed the front of the house. Archie, please, he was saying, and neither the monkey nor the woman seemed to breathe, they held so still.

Bad Archie, said the man, you're a bad, mean monkey.

And when the man's voice had passed the door—Arch-ie! Arch-ie!—when they could hear only crickets in the trees, the old woman stood and looked out to see the organ grinder far up the street, the man calling, stumbling like a drunk in the gutter. The old woman turned to the monkey and smiled and watched him sleeve a butter knife, his thin brown hand taking up his glass by the stem and placing it back down in the ring of wine on the tablecloth.

Now, Archie, she said, and sat again. Where were we?

A STAND OF FABLES

I. Miss Oliana and Her Wish Come to Life

Once upon a time there lived a beautiful young schoolteacher in a fishing village by the sea and all the children adored her. She would enter the class like a source of light, smile her good morning, and begin their arithmetic. Hop-hop! she'd call to them if they dallied. And they rarely dallied.

In the afternoons, as the students scratched their tablets full of compositions, Miss Oliana would stand beside the windows and gaze out over the glittering bay and sea below. It was a grand view, wide with light, and she'd watch the clouds and the shadows of the clouds run in toward the land. She'd watch the fishermen row home, their boats riding deep with fish, and the gulls slow-wheeling overhead.

The years all passed like this, and Miss Oliana found herself teaching the children of her former students. Then she found herself teaching their children's children. Yet never did she despair of these passing years, or the fact that she'd never married or had her own children.

No, if Miss Oliana felt any thorn of regret, it had something to do with those lengthening stares over the water during the quiet, sun-lanced afternoons. And as the children read their compositions from the front of the class, she would feel herself drift back beyond the bay to the hammered-looking sea, to the dull draw of the horizon and the spikes of sunlight.

And the children, so eager to please, would patiently wait for her response, which would be something quick, finally, something that could apply to any child or any essay. And Miss Oliana would scold herself for neglecting these children. She would sit up straight, redouble her attention, and hear not the words this time but the song beneath the words, the small voice so like those before and those to come that they sounded eternal: all that had been being all that would be being all that was.

And she would weep.

And the child at the front of the class would stop, mid-sentence.

And Miss Oliana would touch her eyes, clear her throat, say, Continue, please. It's lovely is all.

And they'd continue, for no one in the village could conceive of a thing contrary to her.

More years passed the same, and more men went to sea. Women cured endless piles of fish, and men drowned and washed ashore as their widows mourned the seasons, which beat relentless and rocking as waves. Storms brought down buildings. Long wars ravaged the inland. Kings gave way to presidents, horses to trucks, boats to planes, letters to telephones, and still nothing changed in the village. The next generations all passed under the watchful eye of the village schoolteacher, Miss Oliana.

As she grew ever more ancient, she also grew more restless for the horizon of which she never tired. She had never heard of so long a life as her own and wondered if something was preventing her passing. In her darker moments she actually suspected the reality of her life: a melody's end is not its goal, but if a melody never finds its end, is it a melody? She worried and she wondered and through the fall and winter these moods persisted as she stared out on the afternoon sea, the children filling notebook after notebook behind her.

What she hoped would pass did not pass. If anything her restlessness grew stronger and more uncomfortable, until she could resist it no longer. She felt pulled almost bodily toward the thin draw of the horizon, and she began to rise each morning before dawn and swim into the bay.

She also began to set her small household in order. She labeled each object—tea kettle, mantel clock, lamp—with the name of its heir, signed her bank account over to the school, and took her secret last farewells of everyone in the village, though none suspected the old woman's designs. She planned to depart unnoticed on the day of the village festival, and soberly she prepared to take leave of her small village and house.

On the night before the festival, Miss Oliana laid out her clothes for the morning and slept lightly as the long trains rumbled heavy into town with circus animals and carnival rides. The men who raised the tents and slaughtered the calves by torchlight were never known for their quiet, reflective ways.

They were loud and boisterous and half-drunk with work and travel and the clean night air and the pretty countrywomen, among other spirits.

But Miss Oliana must have slept, for she woke with the grainy light of morning and went to the shoreline and stowed her towel and clothes on the beach. She looked back at the sleeping gray hills of the village as she greased her body with a thick, herb-scented tallow that would keep her warm.

Then she waded out into the long cold water toward the rising sun, and a swell came to lift her off her feet away from the village.

II. Men and Horses, Hoops and Garters

She'd washed in from the sea long ago, a little orphan girl rowed ashore by a forgotten fisherman who'd found her tangled in his net. The village took her and raised her as one of their own. They didn't tell her how she had come from the sea, her hair all tangles of seaweed and tiny crustaceans and shells.

As the years passed they saw the steady glow of miracle around her. She taught for years and years, but not until she began her strange swims out to sea did the villagers think to show their appreciation. The town elders proposed and organized a special gala in her honor, to be held during the famous summer festival.

It was the custom of the village to play host to a grand festival for the entire country. The event not only proved an economic godsend to the village and its merchants and craftspeople but also brought citizens and entertainers from all across the land to the village.

Word went out. A truly lavish and splendid affair was planned. Master chefs from the city were commissioned; the nation's hybridizers worked to create a new bouquet in her name; pigs were penned beneath apple and pear trees to sweeten them for the slaughter; hot-air balloons were sewn into the shapes of books and inkwells and apples. And, miracle of miracles, the entire affair was kept so hush-hush that Miss Oliana never even suspected such a gala production, let alone one in her honor.

The preparations moved perfectly, as they invariably do when one is performing the right deed. And the day soon came to be, but when the people arrived to carry the guest of honor to the fairgrounds, Miss Oliana did not answer her door.

The door was unlocked, and someone entered the house and found the place tidy, but with no one at home. News spread fast, and if you had been perched above the crowd you'd have seen the whispers sweep over the people. The president stood at the podium and called for a search of the shoreline.

The people all went to the shore, and the ones who had gone into her house found their names on the objects—tea kettle, mantel clock, lamp—and they had taken the things in their arms and cradled them down to the beach where they assembled sadly with the others.

Search parties were formed, men in boats, women along the water's edge, even circus bears combed the woods for the old woman. And the antiques began to warm in the arms of those who held them. The pitcher turned its neck and pursed its lips, as if to speak or cry or who knows what, truly? All the people knew was what they saw — or thought they saw — the old chair crackling as it straightened its back. The clock with its hands to its face, the bewildered little scissors, the grieving bedside lamp.

So totally overcome with fright and awe were the townsfolk that they never noticed the old man rowing in to shore with a boat full of tiny silver fishes. The boat tipped on its keel when the waves nudged it onto the beach, and the tiny fish spilled to the sand with the tinkling sounds of bright silver coins.

III. Sixty Silver Wishes

Anywhere you find timeless fishing villages along the sea, you'll find the same unlucky fisherman who lives alone in his miserable little hovel close to the water. He is a fixture of these towns, a battered old bird against whom all others can take measure and say, There but for the grace of God . . .

And he rows home each dusk with his leaking boat empty of all but a tangled net and the scrap fish that he cleans and cooks for dinner. The village has stopped admiring the decrepit persistence of his folly, has run dry of pity for him, and has developed a taste for ridicule. A grunting old visage he is, of few words and no friends, and children are warned against going near him.

Stories grow around these men like mice from rags or flies from meat, but no one truly knows where they come from or where they go. And so it was in this certain fishing village by the sea that was known through the country for its grand summer festival.

He lived in a miserable hovel close to the sea all alone, and ever since his wife and daughter had died many years ago, he went out to sea every day, regardless of weather or events or anything. He went to the sea each day and fished and fished, and on the day of the fireworks and the circus tents his net felt heavy and full as he tried to haul it aboard, so heavy that he nearly lost his balance and fell into the water. He drew the net to the side of the boat and saw a woman in it. She had long bright hair twisted with seaweed and shells, and he could tell she had been quite beautiful, except her mouth and eyes were swollen with the stings of jellyfish. Her arms and legs were coated with bright fish scales and she glittered in the low clear sunlight.

She smiled up at him and he pulled her into the boat and she said, You have to put me back. She had a smooth and sweet voice and he could only stare at her, rub his eyes, look away.

Return me, she said. Throw me back.

How could I ever? asked the man, looking at her in his net.

Dear fisherman, she said with a sigh. She explained she had no storybook magic for him, nothing to give him, no wishes or favors to grant. Just throw me away, she told him.

She sat up in the bow and began to let herself over the edge of his boat, and for the first time in many years the man saw his life not as it could be but as it was, and his heart sank to the bottom of the sea, where his nets never touched or stirred, and he didn't want to let her go. He said, No—please—just wait.

She waited a moment and smiled and curled herself over the side of his boat. And when the man pulled his net back in, he could hardly lift it aboard. He spilled the tiny fish into the bow of the boat and rowed to shore, feeling stronger by the stroke.

He approached land and heard the sad accordions and the mournful clink of chains as the elephants shifted their feet. The people, more than had ever assembled on the beach, stood holding objects in their arms like magic gifts to the sea. Kettle, clock, comb, and shoe. Lamp, spoon, and cup.

And when the man landed, his boat tipped and all of his fish spread bright like coins. He stepped out of the boat and stood and waited on the shore with all the others who longed dimly for the child girl to wash in from the sea, each wave and gull charged with miracles galore, the world within reach of delight.

TO THE FARM

Funny the things that come back to you. I'm standing in Putnam Supermarket the other day, little old lady just minding my own business, just waiting in line at the deli counter, couple of guys getting sandwiches in front of me, and then all of a sudden past the lobsters I see this other tank all dark and green. Few steps closer, few more, and my stomach goes with the pull—*whole tank filled with eels*—black and squirming against the glass, that raw stink of river and weeds, and this urge rising from inside my throat.

Comes out half laugh, half groan—and the men at the counter turn and smile—I'm over by the tanks at this point, arms open wide to the men, asking them what kind of *person?* I mean, who in their right mind would *eat* these things, anyway?

Guys all grin like I'm a little crazy maybe—which is fine by me, don't care what *anyone* thinks anymore, have come to embrace this cranky-old-woman-ness of mine—man behind the counter wrapping the sandwiches, saying he's had them before, the eels, they're not so bad.

To which I say, *Bahhh!*

And they laugh—and now I drift back—and I start to tell how, once upon a time, back when we lived on the Shetucket River, my husband Bob used to run drop lines off the dock, bits of fresh chicken on the hooks every morning. Who knows, I say, but I think he was thinking turtles. Never caught any fish or turtles that *I* remember. All I know is I'm home from work early one day, sunny summer afternoon down by the water for me, and somehow I get it into my head to see if anything's on the line. Bob's not home, naturally, so I'm there on the dock alone, expecting weeds or bad chicken on the hook, and then something starts fighting and fighting. Line goes all zigzagging and sharp, and I'm pulling it closer and leaning down for one last heave—when *foop!*—this big cold splash wraps itself wet and heavy *around my arm!*

Oh, I start *screaming*—and *keep* screaming—am slapping and hollering at this thing, its head tucking up under my arm. Bob comes rolling into the yard just about here, man running down to the river to me, me gasping to him about snakes, my knees trembling as Bob starts to uncoil the thing from my arm, him laughing how that's no snake, Anna!

Ha, ha, ha, ha, ha—height of fricken hysterical to him—becomes the story of the eel in my bathroom, creature taking up residence for the night, floating almost three foot long, ring of grease on the sides of the tub, and the *musk* of it, Bob asking the eel if she might like some candles and a glass of wine.

Now you *know* I'm a madwoman by morning! Yelling for him to get that effen thing out of my house! Take it up to the farm! Swear I'll pour bleach on it! Swear I'll pour ammonia! Vow great harm upon the eel *and* him!

What a sight I must have been—both then and now—and these guys at the deli are all smiles as I tell this. It's one of those perfect moments in life, everything making brief and beautiful sense in the world, me saying, Sure gotta love an old bitty riled up over *nothing*, don't you?

Sure, sure, they say—and we're all smiling and happy—these guys with their sandwiches asking what happened next?

Well, I say, what d'you *think* happened next? I mean, what d'you think *always* happened next? I tell my husband to get that goddamn creature out of my house, and he rolls his eyes and yeah-yeahs himself off to work early—man never went to work early a day in his *life*—eel looking like she's just gonna loll another day in my bathtub. All comfy, but I've got news for her and pull the plug and go about my business. Get dressed, start laundry, do dishes, whistle while I work, and when I check back on the progress of my eel's death? Can guess what happened next, can't you?

Guys look to one another, shrug they don't know, everyone glancing to the deli meats, the dairy section, entire supermarket leaning close to hear.

Well, I say—and I get all quiet and whispery—when I go back to look, I tell them, *the thing is gone!* Bathtub's empty and I'm standing there as if to calculate the drain, thinking *no fricken way*, no way an eel could fit down that hole. I'm staring as if to put it all together. Greasy ring around my tub, bar of

153

soap in the dish, taste of river in the room, and then *something brushes my feet!*

Oh, I jump and scream all over again — thing lashing itself across the floor toward the toilet — and I'm pure hysteria and go for the paint thinner and Ajax and anything else under the sink that might be harmful. I'm pouring shampoo and rubbing alcohol as Bob comes waltzing home — man forever swooping in for the highlights — says he only ran to the hardware store and flower shop and has, of all things, a bundle of flowers for me.

Laughs in a way that makes the flowers not count for shit — and I throw them back in his face — and Bob goes about scooping the eel into a garbage bag, singsonging that his wife's gone crazy-crazy-crazy-crazy-crazy-crazy-crazy. Laughs his sorry ass up to the farm, where he can clean and cook and choke to death on the bones of the thing for all I care.

Guys in the deli smile and wait for more — but that's all she wrote, I tell them — and soon it's down the cereal aisle they go, leaving me with the deli guy, man behind the counter asking what can he get for me. Half pound of honey ham, I say, half pound of salami, half pound of provolone.

Still have eels on the brain when I get home — the eel, the farm, the house on the Shetucket River, all those years in Baltic washing ashore to me now — time I backed the car over the embankment, way Bob died on the couch, bowl of ice cream on his lap. A person could sit half the night like this, amazed by what returns to them. Pair of porcelain collies on the sill, cuckoo clock over the hutch, wool blanket we used to spread on the grass in the orchard, and who am I to turn any of these things away now? Am half surprised no ghost of Bob comes knocking on the window to let him in.

Or so I say to the kitchen. And the walls, the stove, the whole house holds so still it begins to shiver—that high-pitched hum of glassware in the quiet—and what a strange old shipwreck of a life this is, isn't it? Everything from Bayside to Greenpoint to the farm, all these bits and pieces trailing behind like so much debris. Doily my mother made, old piece of sea glass, cupboard gnawed by a pet raccoon, and what's it all mean in the end?

Can stare the entire night at the light fixture on the ceiling, but that frosted glass, those dead shadows of bugs, none of it's going to help explain anything. The plates, the refrigerator, the sink and faucet, the entire room just wishing the lights were off. The cabinets and doorway trying to will me upstairs already and into bed. The curtains wavering slightly, saying, Get some rest, old woman . . . Wake up and see how you feel in the morning . . . Then go back to the farm if you want . . . Wear that nice skirt and blouse you've been saving . . . Shock the bejeezus out of whoever's left . . .

All right, I say to the house—and the rest of the night has me tossing and turning, sheets and pillows hot to the touch— moonlight on the trees, that shush of leaves in the dark, and over and over in my mind to the farm I go. Keep pulling up to the old house, keep standing in the yard, keep wondering who'll step onto that porch when I arrive—Danny, Margaret, Annie—and I must fall asleep somewhere in all of this, because the next thing I know is sunshine and that sharp green of trees outside. Whatever dreams I had, they disappear at the slightest touch, leaving me tired again, exhausted and heavy, as if I've covered some great distance in the night.

Beautiful day out there—and I get dressed, fix my hair, and start driving to the farm—stop for coffee, stop for gas, and one cool hour of highway to the exit and back roads again. Am forever on the verge of lost as I go—feel I'm trying to catch some dream again, trying to remember some story I read or heard a long time ago—the little church, the truss bridge, the old mills and towns to pass, everything familiar, everything strange, all of it leading to this fork onto Pautipaug Hill, and that déjà vu of cemetery in the gully, and then Bob's stone near the front gate as real as anything else in my life. Can see him gray and shining from half a mile away, like he's been watching all this time for me to pull up.

ROBERT S. CUSSLER
1926–1981

And I get out of the car—why not?—I hereby give myself permission to take this little detour of standing for who knows how long over my old husband like this. Just grass and sky and trees and birds and sunlight and air, and it's days, it's years, it's an entire lifetime before the sound of tires on gravel brings me back to the world, the pop and crackle of pickup truck easing behind, and where am I now as I turn and straighten my skirt? Truck door opening, crunch of boots, and this man asking is that really who he thinks it is?

I stand there—curious to know who I might actually be

156

to him—and he opens his arms and says, Aunt Anna! It's me, Little Leo! Margaret and Leo's son!

To which I say, *That cannot be.*

He smiles in a way that makes me smile and puts his hand to show how tall he must have been last time I saw him—and he hugs me with those easy thick arms of his, old smell of hayloft and cows and kerosene—and he holds me away, this man asking does anyone else know I'm here?

I shake my head—can't seem to speak—Little Leo still this skinny little kid in my mind, his voice still squeaky and sweet as a girl's, that boy inside this disguise of a man some-how. He's saying to come to the farm, saying he'll call Uncle Danny and Aunt Annie, saying he'll see me up at the house, yes? He says all sorts of things that I can't really hear, all of which ends with him telling me to take my time with Uncle Bob.

And after he drives away, sound of his truck tapering up the hill, I turn to Bob and ask if I should just go home. He's under the grass, my husband, but I see him smirk. What, ex-actly, he asks, is *home* again?

Oh, it's true, I say, even *dead* you have to be my nemesis, don't you?

When Bob doesn't say anything next to this, I spit his name and dates to the grass like watermelon seeds. Half of me feels bad for doing this, wants to take it back and say sorry, say I miss him and love him and all that gush—things I feel but never say—but the other half of me just scoffs, raises my face to the sun, takes a deep breath, and starts to the farm.

Up the hill and nothing seems to have changed. The barn,

the house, the cows, the junk trucks in the pasture. Orchard's a bit shaggier than I remember, but the hills, the fields, the light feels the same. Leo steps out of the house—and again that brush of sun and leaves, as if the world's saying everything's going to be all right—and Leo's wife and daughter lovely and smiling beside him, five or six dogs wagging their way across the yard, all of us buoyed gently into the house, that candy-shop smell of hallway and kitchen, counters and sink the same celery green, table in the same place at the windows, brass lamp hanging same as ever from the ceiling.

Bob's brother Danny is on his way, says Leo, and just then Margaret and Ellen and Robert and April arrive together, and all those shotgun questions and jokes begin of how many years has it been? Ten? Twenty? Thirty years gone by? Tell me how does that happen? Honestly, just *how does that happen?*

No one seems to know—though it sure does happen, we say, doesn't it?—and we look at one another in disbelief, last time together being Bob's funeral, Bob's couch sitting in the next room, cushions frowning as if he died there just yesterday, pulmonary embolism, bowl of melted ice cream.

Still no Danny, and we wait and catch one another up on kids and grandkids and bouts with gout, gallbladder operations, and there's the sound of cutlery and ice in glasses as Bob's sister Annie shows up at the door. Leo helps her into the room, her back stooped as she crosses the kitchen, this old woman so much smaller than I remember. It's like hugging a bird cage, all wire and wicker in my arms, two of us trying not to cry as we look at each other, both of us gray and featherless by now, whiskers on her chin, and whiskers I know on mine.

Still no Danny, and Leo sets kielbasa and bread on the table, his wife bringing whiskey and beer and more ice and glasses, everyone drinking to old times and loved ones and how in a flash it all goes by.

Danny arrives, finally, appears like an older version of his brother, that pull of stomach once more, as if Bob himself drifts into the room for a moment, nose battered, hair thin, same yellow sweepstakes smile of his, like he's just won a thousand dollars. We all hurrah for Danny, and soon I'm telling about these *eels* in the supermarket yesterday—*whole tank filled with eels*—which makes us remember the eel in my bathtub, which brings back the time Bob teaches me to drive, me going straight over the embankment, two of us upside-down in the car, windows blown out, slushy sound of glass everywhere, and Bob looking at me, saying I'm trying to *kill* him, aren't I? And I'm like, You idiot, why would I try to kill you in the same car *I'm* driving? We're on the ceiling together, hazards blinking, and he goes, I don't know, Anna, but I'm sure you have your reasons.

Danny seems to recall that there had been some drinking that afternoon, cider always in the cellar those days, Bob always offering to fetch the next pitcher. Even as a kid he'd be downstairs longer and longer, coming back upstairs all dizzy in the head, skinny little boy talking nonsense, sneaking out to sleep with the chickens in the coop.

We laugh—and everything rhymes with everything else—all of us remembering kids up in trees, a rabid coyote to shoot, and Bob driving up to the farm the night of the flood, telling us not to worry, put all our important papers on top of the

159

fridge. And in the morning? You guessed it — whole house gone, swept away, nothing but river — and we stand on the road, Bob rubbing the bristle of his chin. Well, he says, *there goes that*.

Didn't laugh so much back then, but sure can laugh now. Entire afternoon we smile away like this, cheeks sore, and still nothing wrong with one last toast for old times' sake, is there?

Had our day, says Danny, didn't we?

Yes, we did.

It's almost dark as we near the end of this, all of us around the table as the spell slowly lifts. And before anything else can happen, we have all these good nights on the porch to survive, all these hugs and kisses on the lawn to live through. Everyone walks me from the house to my car, the orchard and hills all dark against the sky, dogs like shadows at our feet.

Leo says to come back anytime, always welcome. There's that verge of tears once more, mouth folding down with emotion, and here we go — and this is what breaks my heart — Annie holding my hand in the dark, Danny touching my shoulder, me saying take care, all of us saying goodbye.

Back down the hill again, air plush and soft in the dusk, car heading toward the smell of river and that old gone house of ours. I idle slow where our driveway must have been, place overgrown with vines and trees, water glassy black in the spaces below. Full dark by now, and I pull into what used to be our yard, everything quiet as I stand there. Sky nothing but stars. No moon, no clouds, just so many stars. A truck approaches and passes on the road, everything going dark and quiet again. I lift my skirt and pee into the leaves, sound of steam escaping, wipe with the hem. And how incredible — all the stars, all the trees, all the water moving in the river — so dark and quiet as I lean on the hood of my car for who knows how long. End up driving lost until the middle of the night on these roads. And I'm just so grateful — grateful and happy and tired and amazed — such an incredible sense of gratitude when I make it home at last.